The tension between them was electric, palpable, inevitable

Sam followed Ali into the bedroom. She moved toward the mirror anxiously, glanced at her reflection and said, "I thought I might put my hair up...." Her voice shook, and her hands were clumsy as she picked up her brush.

Sam stepped behind her. "No, please leave it loose." He took a strand between his fingers. Ali's eyes met his in the mirror. She wet her lips with the tip of her tongue. She could feel the heat of his body against her back. Desire, white and hot, flooded through her.

He ran his hand down her bare back, and she shivered. She felt his lips, damp against her shoulder, and then his tongue moving along her neck.

Her knees weak, Ali leaned against him. "Sam, we should talk. We should—"

"We should be making love. That's the only thing we should be doing...."

Dear Reader,

A decade of writing for Temptation! What better way to celebrate than at Christmas—even if Christmas is in July?

In this book, we wanted to present the essence of Christmas—joy and delight, loving and giving—but packaged in a different way. What if the story didn't take place in a winter wonderland? What if the setting were a hot, steamy island in the middle of a heat wave? And to add to the contrariness of the situation, what if both the hero and the heroine *hated* the holiday season, but desperately needed the healing spirit of Christmas to open their hearts to love? This was the challenge of creating *Christmas in July*.

Writing as a team for Temptation, we try to bring our readers something different in each book. Our tenth year has been very special for us—beginning with our first time-travel romance, *The Pirate's Woman,* a Waldenbooks bestseller, and ending with *The Trouble with Babies,* a romantic romp due out soon.

We are deeply grateful to our editors for the opportunity to tell our stories, and we wish Temptation a glorious tenth anniversary. Here's to many more!

And to each of our readers, a heartfelt thank-you and a very Merry Christmas in July.

Madeline Harper

(Shannon Harper & Madeline Porter)

CHRISTMAS IN JULY

MADELINE HARPER

Harlequin Books

TORONTO • NEW YORK • LONDON
AMSTERDAM • PARIS • SYDNEY • HAMBURG
STOCKHOLM • ATHENS • TOKYO • MILAN
MADRID • WARSAW • BUDAPEST • AUCKLAND

To all who cherish Christmas in their hearts year-round

ISBN 0-373-25599-3

CHRISTMAS IN JULY

Copyright © 1994 by Madeline Porter and Shannon Harper.

1

SAM CANTRELL TOOK OFF the jacket of his khaki suit and slung it over his shoulder. He was more concerned about the heat than the bulge made by the holster under his arm. One thing was for damn sure—there wasn't anyone around to see his gun.

He'd assumed that there'd be taxi service on Indigo Isle, but he'd been wrong. No taxi, no car rental. No people. Nothing but a long road of crushed shell leading down a corridor of live oaks that dripped with Spanish moss. Gnats seemed attracted to the moss—and to Sam. He swatted away a swarm, wiped the perspiration from his eyes and trudged on.

He had a job to do and the heat and humidity of this island off the coast of South Carolina was only an irritant. He expected there'd be many more before the case was over. So he ignored the sweat stains on his pale blue shirt and gave no heed to the leather holster that was almost a part of his body.

Sam loosened his tie and ran a hand through his dark hair as he rounded a bend in the road. That's when he saw the sign.

SPICE OF LIFE
Private Property
KEEP OUT

Sam kept on walking.

He crossed the road, climbed a hill to the wide yard and approached a row of low buildings with glass roofs—the Spice of Life greenhouses. He walked up to the closest building carefully, cautiously. Then he stopped, his back flattened against the wooden siding. He peered inside. There was no one, nothing. Only plants, unrecognizable to Sam. He moved to the next window, and then the next.

He crouched low, creeping along the length of the greenhouse, stopping to look inside, moving on. He was beginning to feel like an idiot. There were times to play it cool, times to stand and take a chance. Sam stood.

That's when he saw her, a woman slipping between the tables and among the plants.

He watched her for a long moment. She didn't *look* like a criminal, but he knew looks could be deceiving. Still, she seemed wholesome enough with her straight brown hair pulled back carelessly in a ponytail, her face shiny from the heat and devoid of makeup. He shook his head. Alicia Paxton Bell wasn't what he had expected.

She walked along the rows of plants, stopping to pull at her very short shorts, which had caught on a nail. He smiled at the view of her long tanned legs as he watched her tug. Yep, wholesome but sexy—a hell of a combination. It didn't fit his preconceived image at all. She was hardly the cosmopolitan woman whose photos he'd seen. For a moment Sam wondered if he was in the right place.

Of course he was. This was the Spice of Life company; the woman inside was Alicia Paxton Bell. It was time to act. He stepped away from the window, put his jacket on, picked up his canvas bag and headed toward the front of the greenhouse.

He thought about knocking on the greenhouse door and then changed his mind. While she was fooling with her plants at the other end of the building, he might as well have a look around.

He stepped inside and felt instant relief. Huge fans blew the tepid air over tables lined with potted plants. Sam took a deep breath. The air was heavy with scents he couldn't identify. He knew they were herbs—obviously—or maybe spices, but he had no idea which ones. To Sam they just smelled tangy.

There was a worktable nestled in the corner of the greenhouse. He walked over and checked it out quickly. Scrawled lists, inventories, her initials. He waited. Alicia Paxton Bell would be here soon. It didn't take a detective to figure that out.

ALI WAS WATERING POTS of sun-loving rosemary when she heard a noise in the front of the greenhouse. She froze and waited. She hadn't been told to expect visitors at Spice of Life today, but someone was in the building. She wondered what had happened to the damned watchdogs. They were never around when she needed them.

Her cousins were up at the big house, as they called the family home, and their son, Brian, was playing softball

with friends. It was her responsibility to handle the intruder.

Dragging the hose along after her, Ali crept toward the
front of Greenhouse One. Barefoot, she moved silently
along the sandy path, her finger on the trigger of the
spray nozzle. It wasn't exactly a weapon, but it was all
she had.

Warily, she peered over a table of empty clay pots. The
greenhouse was quiet with row after row of basil, oreg-
ano, thyme and coriander warmed by sunlight pouring
through the glass roof. Nothing unusual there.

Then she saw him, skulking around her cousin's
worktable. She had an immediate impression of a tall,
dark-haired man whose broad shoulders strained at the
confines of his khaki jacket. He looked big and tough,
like someone who didn't belong here. Danger signals
prickled along her spine.

"Hey, you!"

He turned toward her in a half crouch, balanced on the
balls of his feet, quick and catlike.

Acting on instinct, Ali aimed the hose and pulled the
trigger. The spray hit him full force. "This property and
this greenhouse are off-limits. You're breaking the law,
and you have ten seconds to clear out!"

Sam had expected almost anything but this. A real
weapon might not have surprised him, but the sudden
cold shower threw him off totally. It also cooled him,
which wasn't exactly unwelcome.

But enough was enough. "Turn off the water! I sur-
render!"

She took her finger off the trigger, and Sam was reprieved. He shook himself, scattering water all around. His hair was plastered to his head, his shirt and jacket were soaked and water dripped into his shoes. He touched the holster tentatively, shrugged in his jacket so it wouldn't be noticeable. Later he would put it away. Whatever her agenda, it wasn't threatening. He didn't need a gun against her hose!

"Now you have five seconds," she warned, lifting the nozzle again.

Sam reached in his pants pocket for a handkerchief that was at least partially dry. He took his time wiping his face and thought about how to play the scene. The woman had sneaked up on him and actually gained the upper hand, which should have irritated him, but somehow it didn't. Besides, he had no desire to get into a confrontation, make her even angrier and get kicked off the island. That would defeat his purpose.

"Do you always greet your guests in such a friendly fashion?" he asked.

"You're not a guest. As far as I know," she snapped, then aimed her hose. "And your time is up."

"Isn't a man supposed to be innocent until proven guilty? I could very well be here for a legitimate purpose—"

"Not likely. And even so, our greenhouses are still off-limits."

Sam gritted his teeth and ignored the determination in her deep brown eyes. He disliked people who interrupted. "Maybe if you'd listen to what I have to say—"

"Are you from the press? Is that it? I thought I knew all of the news vultures—"

"Now it's my turn to interrupt you," Sam announced. "I'm not a newsman, I'm a—"

"Spy? Step away from that workbench! My cousin Tiger might have left some of his notes out."

"Spy?" That hit close to home. He could feel the muscles in his jaw tense as he gazed at her through narrowed eyes. What did she know?

"Industrial-type spy. Since Spice of Life began coming on so strong, more than one rival has been after our formula for low-country gumbo mix."

Sam smiled with relief. "A spice spy? Yeah, I like that idea. Okay. I'm a spice spy. Got any hot tips on thyme?"

Her eyes narrowed. "It's pronounced 'time.' The *h* is silent. You obviously know nothing about herbs," she said dismissively. "So if you're not a spy, what are you, some nut with a warped sense of humor? I want to see your ID. Now."

"You're kidding."

"I've never been more serious," she told him.

"What is this island, some private domain where you make up the rules?"

"As a matter of fact, it is. My cousin and his wife own Indigo Isle, and we don't let just anyone come here. How'd you get on the ferry? And more importantly, what made Captain Poteet let you off at Indigo?"

"If you'll aim your weapon the other way, I'll show you," Sam said. "I have a letter here." He fished in his pocket and pulled out a wilted envelope. "In it your cousin Mr. Thomas Mallory said—"

"Nobody around here calls me Thomas."

Sam and Ali both turned toward the voice. A couple stood in the doorway. The man was short, middle-aged and balding with a round face that radiated good cheer. The woman with him was a little younger, a little shorter and much thinner with curling reddish hair and a nose full of freckles.

"I'm known as Tiger," the man said. "And this is my wife, Gwen. You must be that friend of Billy Smithson's, the one who's renting Flattop. I guess you've met my cousin Ali Paxton."

Sam nodded politely.

"Son, you're wetter than a drowned rat," Tiger commented. "What happened to you? Walk under one of our sprinklers?"

"Not exactly," Sam answered. He raised an eyebrow in Ali's direction. "I was greeted by a welcoming committee."

Ali didn't lower her eyes or look embarrassed. Instead, she responded with a little shrug. "I had no idea who he was. So I turned the hose on him."

Gwen Mallory put her hand over her mouth to bite back laughter. Tiger's eyes twinkled, too, although he kept a straight face. "Now, Ali, honey, that's no way to greet a paying guest."

"I didn't know he was renting Flattop. I thought he was a reporter. Or maybe a spy. He was skulking around like a fox."

"Hey, just a minute," Sam spoke up. "I wasn't skulking! I don't even know how to skulk. I was lost and looking for directions when the guard here—" he gestured toward Ali "—turned the hose on me. And what is this Flattop, anyway?"

Ali pointed to the worktable. "He was going through the papers. If that's not skulking and spying, I don't know what is."

Sam smiled an innocent, ingratiating smile. "I was trying to find out if I was in the right place. I thought if I saw Mr. Mallory's...I mean Tiger's...name on something, I'd have a clue. I didn't take anything." He allowed defensiveness to creep into his voice—a nice touch, he thought.

"Of course you didn't," Gwen said. "It's our fault for not telling Ali we were putting you in Flattop."

"What *is* Flattop?" Sam asked again.

"That's the beach cottage you're renting," Tiger answered.

"It's a right nice place, but it has a flat roof, and it's not all that high," Gwen added. "You're so tall you can probably touch the ceiling. But I know you'll love it anyway."

"I'm sure I will," Sam said unconvincingly.

"It's ready, even though we didn't expect you so soon. That's why there was no one to meet the ferry. You do forgive us, don't you?"

Sam nodded graciously. "Mrs. Mallory, with a smile like that, I'd forgive you anything."

He turned up the volume of his own smile and noted Gwen's quick flush of pleasure. Then out of the corner of his eye he caught the look on Ali's face. Her lip curled disdainfully, and her expression spoke volumes. Cousin Gwen might be susceptible to flattery and charm, but it wouldn't work on Ali.

That only made Sam more determined.

"So who is he?" Ali asked. "And why's he here?"

"My name's Sam Cantrell, and I'm renting one of your cottages, the one called Flattop—" he smiled again at Gwen "—for the month of July."

Ali arched her eyebrows. "Why would you come to Indigo Isle in July? It's forty times hotter than Hades here, and anyone with any sense is in the mountains. That's where we'd be if we didn't have a business to run. So why're you—?"

"I'm sure he has his reasons," Gwen soothed. "Now, no more third degree, Ali. He's not on trial. What about your luggage, Mr. Cantrell? Surely you have more than that one bag."

"Yes, I have others down at the dock. I thought I could get a taxi."

Tiger and Gwen laughed, and Ali allowed herself a little smirk.

"I'll get the pickup and go after your luggage," Tiger offered. "Come along with me. Afterward, I'll drop you off at Flattop. You probably want to change."

"I'm sure you'll enjoy Flattop," Gwen said. "It's smack-dab on the beach and not far from the cottage where Ali lives."

"How convenient," Sam murmured under his breath. "I mean, how scenic. I'm sure that I'll enjoy watching, uh, the sun set over the ocean."

"Too bad," Ali piped up. "Our cottages face the east."

"Then I guess I'll enjoy the sun *rising* over the ocean."

Sam's eyes met Ali's and held in a moment of unspoken challenge. She was tall, sexy, attractive and about as approachable as a rattlesnake. She wasn't going to be easy, this Alicia Paxton Bell, but he was a man of patience and skill.

Ali looked away first. "I have work to do. Enjoy your stay, Mr. . . . ."

"Cantrell. Sam Cantrell. I hope you'll call me Sam, Ali."

She looked away toward Gwen. "The basil in the other greenhouse needs to be topped. I'll see to it." She turned on her heel and was gone.

Tiger looked apologetic, but Gwen took over. "You'll have to excuse Ali. She's a wonderful person and a great help to us. I don't know what we'd do without her. Maybe she's a bit impetuous. Oh, all right, she's a regular firebrand."

"Gwen," Tiger interrupted.

"Oh, I know. You don't want to hear about Ali or our little business, do you, Mr. Cantrell?"

"Call me Sam, please."

"What you really want to do is get settled in, don't you, Sam?" Gwen was all Southern graciousness.

Actually, Sam *did* want to hear about Ali, but he knew that the first hour of his arrival wasn't the time to seem interested. It could wait.

"Come on," Tiger said. "Let's get your luggage, Sam. There's a store of sorts down at the gas station. You can get supplies there."

"Supplies?"

"You know, groceries, staples, all that stuff. If there's something special you need, we can order from the mainland."

Sam's shoulders sagged. He'd hoped for a restaurant where he could enjoy a decent meal, only to find he'd have to buy his own groceries—at a gas station!

"How many families live here?" he asked.

"Oh, couple of dozen," Tiger informed him. "Now, some of 'em are pretty extended—sisters, brothers, cousins and such. Year-round population is about fifty or so. Almost everyone works for us. Except the Loomis family. They run the gas station and post office. During the season we rent out our cottages. We have four, but you and Ali are our only tenants now. 'Course, she's not really a tenant, but she prefers to live on her own instead of with us up at the big house."

"You have to come and visit," Gwen invited. "We'd welcome you for dinner any night."

"I'd like that," Sam answered, thinking that the sooner the invitation was extended, the better.

"Well, come along, Sam," Tiger urged. "We need to get moving out toward the dock to collect your luggage. Can't leave all the work to the women."

ALI PICKED CAREFULLY through the just-harvested basil leaves. They'd dry naturally, in the sun, and then be blended with other herbs and spices into one of Tiger's specialty herb mixtures that were packaged under the Spice of Life label. The product was sold to gourmet stores from Atlanta to Boston, where Carolina low-country cooking was becoming a fad.

She looked up as Gwen came in and settled beside her on the workbench. "So, tell me what you think."

"About what?" Ali equivocated.

"About him. About Sam Cantrell. I almost had a laughing fit when I saw what you'd done to him! Ali, how could you?"

"He was an intruder."

"So you turned the hose on him?" Gwen asked.

"What did you expect? I had no idea who he was. For all I know he could have been...a spice spy—or worse."

Gwen laughed. "Well, he's not, and I truly apologize for not telling you that we rented Flattop to Sam Cantrell. We're not very good organizers, Tiger and me. That's why we need you to make sure that Spice of Life is up to speed."

"It doesn't matter. He's here. I couldn't run him away," Ali said matter-of-factly. "Even though I tried."

Gwen set about helping her sort through the leaves. She didn't look up as she went on about Sam. "He's very handsome, isn't he? And he has an awfully nice physique."

"I didn't notice." Ali, too, kept her head down, eyes on the basil.

"How could you not notice? That broad chest, the long legs, the—"

"Gwen Mallory! Shame on you and your prurient interests," Ali teased. "Why, you're a married woman."

"Married but not dead. Isn't that the old joke? And I repeat, he really is handsome."

"Umm." Ali tried to be noncommittal. In fact, she *had* noticed how good-looking Sam Cantrell was. Tall, at least six foot two, half a foot taller than Ali's own five foot eight. Green eyes. Dark brown, almost black hair. No doubt about it, he was a hunk, but that didn't mean Ali was going to drop her guard. She continued working on the basil.

"He seems in awfully good shape, which surprises me," her cousin said thoughtfully.

Ali looked up from the basil leaves. "Why in the world would you be surprised at that?"

"Because when Billy recommended him to Tiger—he was a friend of a friend—he told us that Sam needed a place to rest and recuperate. He'd been ill or run-down, I can't exactly remember which. But he doesn't look at all sick to me. Does he to you?"

Ali shook her head firmly. "Not one bit."

In fact, she thought Sam Cantrell looked very healthy indeed. Healthy, sexy, dangerous. She'd sensed the danger the minute she'd laid eyes on him. The hard, tough lines of his body, the threatening crouch. He'd seemed so purposeful, not like a casual visitor. No wonder she'd acted so instinctively with the hose.

"He doesn't look to me like the kind of man who belongs on Indigo Isle."

"Lots of folks from Atlanta and Charleston rent cottages."

"He's different, Gwen."

"Different? Better looking than most, that's for sure."

Ali sighed and struggled to put her feelings into words. "Maybe it's the way he walks...."

Gwen hooted with laughter. "If you noticed the way he walks, you *were* paying attention."

"I was suspicious, so I watched him. Closely," Ali defended. "He just stalked around so damned arrogantly."

"You told us he skulked."

"Skulked, stalked... whatever. And when he smiles his eyes stay the same. Kind of hard and cold and measuring. I guarantee all that charm is an act."

"I think his smile is wonder—"

Ali interrupted. "How long did you say he was going to be here?"

"I didn't say, but he did, remember? He'll be renting the cabin for all of July."

A month. A long, hot, steamy month with Sam Cantrell in the cottage next to hers. Ali was thoughtful for a moment before she commented, "Gwen, there's something about Sam Cantrell—"

Two barking dogs and a ten-year-old boy tore into the greenhouse. By a miracle of maneuvering and sidestepping, the trio somehow avoided the pot-laden tables.

"Well, *now* you're here, Brian," Ali said in mock anger. "Where were the watchdogs when I needed them?"

The two wet and sandy Labrador retrievers wiggled and quivered in excitement at Ali's feet. Their tails flopped heavily and long red tongues lolled out of their open mouths.

"We were all down at the beach after our ball game," the boy said. "Did you need us? You could have called," he continued, not waiting for a response. "Max and Jinx and I would have been here in a shot. We'd have chased the bad guys away."

The dogs rolled on their backs and squirmed with joy at the attention.

"Fine watchdogs," Ali muttered.

"Shh," Brian cautioned. "They'll hear you."

"Good. Maybe that'll make them repentant for not being here to protect me."

"From the bad guys?" Brian asked.

"There aren't any bad guys around," Gwen announced to her son. "Now take those dogs away, hose them off and then get yourself into the shower."

"What's for dinner?" Brian asked. "I'm starving."

"Ask your father. He's the cook," Gwen called out to the boy's retreating back. Then, turning to Ali, she scolded, "It's not wise to jump to conclusions. These suspicions of yours aren't healthy."

Ali looked perplexed.

"You know what I'm talking about—referring to Sam as a bad guy. It's not healthy, Alicia."

"Yes, Gwendolyn," Ali mimicked. She always knew that Gwen was serious when she used her full name. "I know I'm suspicious, but I have a right to be after all the

press I've dodged. I never know when someone is going
to show up and start asking about Casey again or bring
up the missing money."

"Ali, honey—"

"You know as well as I do that those damned reporters never give up. Maybe in time I'll relax and trust people again, but not for a while."

"Well, you know best about that," Gwen said mildly.
"But I still like Sam Cantrell's looks."

"Looks can be deceiving," Ali said dourly.

"I suppose they can."

The two women sat in silence for a while.

"I do wonder why he's really here," Ali said finally.

"Why don't you find out? Take him on as a project."

"I have plenty of projects, Gwen. Plans for our booth
at the Trade Mart in Atlanta, layout for the new Spice of
Life catalog, brochures, ads, press releases—"

"But no plans to come to Atlanta and be with us for
the Christmas show?"

"You know how I feel about the holidays since
Casey. . . since he left."

Gwen reached out and squeezed Ali's hand. "'Course
I do, honey. But this won't be anything like a holiday
season. It'll just be make-believe Christmas in the middle of the summer."

"Christmas in July at the trade show has all the trap-
pings of Christmas in December, and I don't want any
part of it."

"I hear you," Gwen replied with a sigh. "But I still think your attitude could use some overhauling. Not just about Christmas but about Sam Cantrell, too. Despite what you say, he has an awfully nice smile," she went on, undaunted. "I wonder how he'd look in a bathing suit?"

"Gwen—"

Gwen cut her eyes toward Ali. "Bet you wonder, too."

Ali sniffed disdainfully. "I have much more on my mind than worrying about Sam Whoever in a bathing suit."

"Time will tell," Gwen murmured.

"Do you always have to get the last word?" Ali was on the verge of exasperation.

"It's a skill I've acquired after years of dealing with you and Tiger."

Ali got up abruptly. "I'm going up to the office and get some work done. Alone. With no one to talk to me about great physiques and green eyes."

"I never mentioned his green eyes, Ali."

Hiding her embarrassment, Ali turned at the door and said darkly, "I think it's a big mistake to let strangers on the island."

"I like what he's accomplished already," Gwen replied.

"What are you talking about? He just arrived."

"Never mind that. He's made a big impression on you, Ali. I haven't seen you this stirred up over a man—"

Ali turned on her heel and went out the door toward the big house and her office.

"Welcome back to the real world," Gwen called after her.

2

SAM HADN'T MEANT TO WATCH the sun rise over Indigo Isle. He was a man who liked late nights and lazy mornings, but Ali's words must have challenged his unconscious because he was wide-awake and rolling out of bed the next day at 6:00 a.m.

What a view, Sam thought as he took his mug of instant coffee onto the screened porch and watched the light shimmer across the ocean. It was a spectacular sight, turning the blackness red, orange and then pink as dawn broke.

To the south along the beach he could see the cottage that had been in darkness last night until Ali came home. He'd been sitting here on the porch, swatting mosquitoes and doing a little surreptitious spying, when she got in late and went right to bed. Or at least the lights had gone out immediately. Not one for smearing on a lot of night creams, he decided.

That would have surprised Sam up until yesterday. Before he met her, Sam thought he knew a great deal about Alicia Paxton Bell. He'd researched her well through newspaper clippings and interviews conducted in Atlanta before he headed for Indigo Isle. He'd learned she was smart, attractive, well educated. After college she and her husband, Casey Bell, had hit Atlanta like twin tornadoes, both securing high-profile positions.

Ali had found work in public relations with the city tourist bureau. Atlanta had a lot to offer—a winning professional baseball team, an enviable site for the Olympics and the perfect location for new industry. The bustling city took tourism seriously, and so had Ali. Her success had been phenomenal—until the scandal, the day her husband had walked away from his company with half a million dollars.

Sam was aware that thirdhand accounts weren't as good as firsthand information. He'd get that now. He had the perfect setup, living next to her on the beach, but he needed to circumvent her defenses in order to find out more about Ali.

That was a problem. She seemed to be equipped with lots and lots of defenses, like that back-to-nature role she was playing. It just didn't jibe with all the information he had about her from Atlanta, where she'd had a high-living life-style and marriage. Indigo Isle was a good cover, but he could see through it. Experience had taught him that most people weren't what they seemed, and just because a woman chose to avoid night cream it didn't make her honest.

Sam's profession made him not only suspicious but cynical, but that went with the territory. People in his field didn't usually meet and mingle with society's most upstanding citizens. Of course, his job was a hell of a lot better than a lot of others.

He'd rather be a private investigator than a cop.

In his private-eye job Sam was off the street, relatively safe, dealing with white-collar crime. He took the cases that law enforcement put on the back burner or those that publicity-conscious citizens wanted handled privately, without police involvement.

Some of the cases included a wealthy wife blackmailed by her lover, an office manager heading for Mexico with the company payroll, a dubious businessman who wanted to retrieve the stocks and bonds stolen from his home safe. Sam and his partner were discreet with a high degree of success. Usually the only danger Sam faced was being found out before the time was right.

Sam's lips curved in a grin. The physical danger of this case was negligible. Ali already had taken her best shot at him with her menacing spray, and he'd survived that. As soon as he had moved into Flattop he'd put his gun and holster away. Now the challenge was to play his cards right and stay one step ahead of his suspect. Armed with nothing more than a neighborly request, he was going to face Ali in the bright morning sunlight.

Barefoot, in shorts and a T-shirt, coffee cup in hand, he headed for her cottage. The sandy path from the beach led up to her front porch, but when he saw movement and a light in the kitchen, he veered off the path and took a shortcut across the yard.

"Damn!" He'd gone only a couple of steps when something stung the bottom of his bare foot, sending a stabbing pain right through him. "Damn," he repeated, "what the hell—?" Hopping around on one foot, his coffee sloshing, Sam succeeded only in getting stung on the bottom of his other foot. It was hopeless. For a moment he stood immobile, wondering what had attacked him, swatting around at imaginary insects.

"They're sandspurs," Ali called out as she stepped onto the back porch, smirking just a little, Sam noticed in spite of his pain. "Swatting won't help. Don't sit down!" she cautioned.

"I'm not sitting down." He continued to hop around on one foot while he pulled out the round prickly spur and then cautiously changed feet to repeat the operation, his coffee a thing of the past.

"Walk on the sand path," she cautioned. "Everyone knows to wear shoes if you go in the yard."

"Everyone?"

"Everyone who comes to Indigo Isle. Didn't your good friend Billy tell you?" she asked innocently.

"No, he didn't. Obviously there was a lot I wasn't told. Like no restaurant, no taxis, no bars, no air-conditioning, no cable TV, no liquor store—"

"Are you an alcoholic?"

"What?" He was balanced on one foot, afraid to put the other one down.

"Most of what you miss seems to involve booze."

"Must be the heat, the bugs, the sandspurs and a very low ceiling. Those things can drive a man to drink."

"Well, I suppose you can come on over," she offered reluctantly.

"How do you suggest I get there?"

"You could always keep on going and hope for the best."

"Kind of like walking through a mine field."

"No, there's a lot more chance you'll pick up a sand-spur than hit a mine. They're small round burrs and they have sharp spikes."

"I know what they are now. Thanks," he said sarcastically. He retraced his steps, picking up only one more spur. "I can hardly feel the pain," he said, pulling it from the heel of his foot and then continuing along the path to her back porch.

"I don't think you're finding our island to your liking, ah, Mr...."

Sam could have sworn she was enjoying his discomfort. He saw a perverse satisfaction in her eyes.

"Sam," he said flatly. "And you're wrong. I'm very fond of this island, Ali. In fact, I might just stay all summer." He walked confidently toward her, meeting her eyes challengingly. It was easy to emit confidence when he knew there weren't any more sandspurs to contend with.

Sam paused at the bottom of the steps and gazed up at Ali. Her hair was loose and flowing around her shoulders, straight and shiny brown, glowing in the dawn's light. He could tell she'd just blown it dry. There were still a few darkly damp strands among those that shone golden. There were golden lights in her eyes, too. She was dressed casually, like Sam, in shorts and a T-shirt, but where he felt unkempt and sloppy, she looked very much together. She was a hell of a sexy-looking woman, but with an easygoing, I-don't-give-a-damn attitude.

Despite his real reasons for being on Indigo Isle, he couldn't help but look at her. She was something to see, and he was a man with eyes. The attraction was there. Sam determined to make it work for him and his case.

He smiled his most disarming smile, one—he'd been told—that could melt icebergs with its warmth.

It didn't work with Ali. She looked at him coolly, and she didn't smile back.

Sam tried another approach—straightforwardness. "Yesterday I think we got off on the wrong foot."

"My, you have a way with words," Ali commented.

"All right, let's keep my foot out of it. We're neighbors, and I want . . . I'd like to—"

"Apology accepted."

Sam frowned. He'd expected *her* to apologize! "Wait a minute. You turned the hose on me."

"You were trespassing," she reminded him.

He searched for a defense and came up empty. "All right, I apologize for whatever I did."

"Apology accepted," she repeated as she turned to go into the house.

"What about my sugar?" he called out. "I came over to borrow a spoonful of sugar."

Ali stepped back onto the porch. "A *spoonful* of sugar?"

"Just enough for a cup of coffee, that's all I ask." He was appropriately polite even though he didn't expect the attitude to impress Ali. "I went to that little grocery store, but I forgot sugar. I plan to go back later." In truth, he didn't use sugar or cream, but Ali couldn't know that. "And I figured Loomis didn't deliver."

Sam was pleased to see her laugh, a sparkling sound that glittered like sunlight on the sea.

"Hardly," she said. "Come on in. I'll give you a spoonful." She held the door open and closed it after him. As he walked past her their arms touched. It was the first time he'd been close to her, the first time he'd made contact. He could smell the scent of her freshly shampooed hair. Flowers. Sunshine. Summer.

Watch it, he warned himself. This was a fact-finding mission, not an early-morning rendezvous, but he was finding the physical appeal of Ali Paxton Bell as compelling as the intellectual chase.

The kitchen of her cottage was similar to Sam's except that she'd brightened it with posters and watercolors and, of course, the ceiling was higher. "This is nice, I—"

"Thanks." Ali didn't let him get into a discussion of her kitchen. Sam was the only man except Tiger who'd been in Ali's cottage, and he seemed to fill the room with his maleness. With his tousled hair, sleepy eyes and bare feet, his presence signaled an intimacy that made her uneasy. But then, everything about Sam Cantrell kept her on edge. The heavy air seemed to vibrate with his presence. She'd been foolish to invite him in.

"Here's your sugar," she said abruptly. She handed him a half-filled bowl. "Anything else?" Her eyes met his evenly.

"Oh, yes. I can think of lots of things, Ali." He turned up the incandescence of his smile.

The promise of possibilities shimmered in the July sunshine. His eyes, no longer sleepy, challenged her with a sexy awareness. Ali felt her breath quicken and heat rise to her cheeks. Irritated at her reaction, she tore her eyes from his and made a show of looking at her watch.

"Sorry. Sugar is all I have to offer. Work starts early for me, before it gets too hot. So . . ." She took two long strides toward the door, opened it and waited.

"Now I have the sugar but no coffee."

She frowned, and he held up his empty cup. "I lost all of it on the way over. A refill would be the friendly thing to do."

Without comment, Ali picked up her coffeepot and filled Sam's cup, instinctively keeping him at arm's length.

He took a sip. "Great."

"You take it black?" She leaned stiffly against the kitchen counter, warily watching him.

"Yes."

"No milk?"

Sam shook his head.

"No sugar?"

"No—uh, yes, of course." He put his cup on the counter and poured in a little sugar from the bowl.

Ali handed him a spoon, and he stirred almost ceremoniously. "Well, thanks for the coffee." He took a sip and grimaced slightly. "Just the way I like it."

"Is that so?" Ali raised a skeptical eyebrow. "Then mission accomplished. So long, Sam."

But he wasn't that easily dismissed. He lounged against the counter, cradling the cup, seemingly at ease in *her* kitchen. "So," he asked, "what is there to do around here?"

"You're doing it, Sam," she said flatly. "Enjoying the fresh air and sea breeze. Indigo Isle is going to be very boring for a man like you."

He chuckled, low and softly, a sound that momentarily put her off guard. "A man like me? Sounds like you've been thinking about me, Ali. A man like me," he repeated slowly.

"Not at all," she lied. "I simply meant Indigo Isle is not exactly Atlanta. It's hardly the place for you."

He shrugged. "How do you know that when you don't know me? Maybe you should take the time to find out what I'm really like. How about dinner one evening? I'll cook," he offered.

"I don't have much time for a social life." She opened the screen door. "The business keeps me occupied."

"That's too bad, but who knows...things change, and I do have time. Lots of time." He flashed another dazzling smile, but Ali was watching his eyes. Cool, green and calculating.

Sam went out and then turned to look back at her through the screen. "So long, then, and thanks again." He went down the stairs with his cup of coffee and bowl of sugar and headed down the path.

Ali watched him thoughtfully through the screen door, wondering what that visit was all about. On the surface it seemed obvious. Sam was a guy on the make, cozying up to his neighbor, hoping for some summer fun.

But there was something more. Instinctively she knew it. She couldn't shake her feelings about him. Supposedly he'd come to Indigo Isle to recuperate, but he looked healthy and strong; in fact, he exuded masculinity. And sex appeal. Even early in the morning. *Especially* early in the morning.

Ali poured a cup of coffee. She wished she could stop obsessing about him and accept him at face value, but she couldn't. Sam was like a damned sandspur, prickly, irritating and almost impossible to shake off.

She was being overly suspicious, as she always was of anyone outside her family. But why not, considering what had happened to her? What woman wouldn't put up a protective front after her life had been snatched away by a man who swore he loved her?

Ali's fingers tightened on the mug as her mind flashed back. Casey had been her college sweetheart, the first man she'd ever loved, her knight in shining armor. She had imbued him with all her youthful longings, her fantasies, her hopes. They were the perfect couple, or so everyone believed. Young, rich, in love. They had the world at their feet.

Then her idol showed his true colors, and did it at a time and in a way that made it even more despicable. One day her life was perfect; the next day it was a living hell. She lost everything. Casey. Her house. Her job. And her good name. The loss had been hard to bear, but the public airing of her failure had been devastating, as her fairy-tale marriage was held up to the world as nothing but a sham. Stripped of her dignity, she'd run to Indigo.

Ali took a sip of her coffee. It tasted cold and bitter in her mouth. She poured it down the drain and rinsed her cup. She wasn't going to think of Casey—or of Sam Cantrell. She had to keep moving forward, one step at a time. And the next step was the Spice of Life brochure for the Christmas trade show in Atlanta.

Her lips quirked in a sardonic smile. There it was again. Christmas. Even in her thoughts, she couldn't get away from it.

SAM'S DAY, which hadn't started out all that well, continued downhill as he went off on a little Ali fact-finding expedition. Tate Loomis at the gas station and grocery store was interested in talking, all right—about everything but Ali Paxton Bell. A longtime resident of Indigo Isle, Loomis knew all about fishing, crabbing, shrimping, tides, winds and currents. He was an expert on the history of the island, from the first Mallory settlement in the 1840s as indigo farmers, to Tiger, who'd come back home five years earlier.

"Who would've thought it," Tate asked, pipe clamped between his teeth, feet on the porch rail, "that Tiger'd give up his law practice and come back to Indigo Isle when his momma died? He don't know diddly about farming, not even raisin' those puny little herbs—at first. 'Course, Gwen was a farmer's daughter, raised in the

South Car'lina up-country. She taught him how to grow just about anythin'."

"So what about the young woman who's working out there with them—Ali, I think her name is." Sam took a swig of the ice-cold drink he'd pulled out of Loomis's cooler.

"Yep, that's Ali, a fine gal. Her momma and Tiger's daddy was sister and brother. Which makes Ali and Tiger first cousins, you see?" The question didn't require a response; it was Loomis's way of speaking. "She grew up on the mainland," he added with a nod in the direction of Charleston. "But that didn't do her no harm." His wide girth shook with laughter.

Sam nonchalantly studied the tips of his running shoes. "About how long has she been back here?"

"Long enough. Why you interested in that, son?"

"Just curiosity, I guess. She's a good-looking woman."

"That she is. I've known Ali since she was knee-high to a grasshopper. She's a fine gal. Everyone on the island knows that."

Sam rocked silently beside Loomis for a while. "I understand she's a widow?"

"Yep."

Sam waited for more. What he got was an obvious dismissal. "No finer family than the Mallorys and their kin." Loomis stood creakily. "I'll be seeing you."

Captain Poteet was equally noncommittal. He ran the twice-daily ferry over to the mainland, but he wasn't willing to discuss the reasons for Ali's return to Indigo Isle. And the casual conversation Sam started with a couple of women fishing off the pier got him nowhere, either. Everyone loved Ali. She was a possible candidate for sainthood.

There was no mention by anyone of Casey Bell or the fact that he'd absconded with half a million dollars from his Atlanta company or that authorities believed Ali had inside information about where the money was hidden.

Sam couldn't figure it. As far as he was concerned, Ali's behavior was highly suspicious. She'd bolted from Atlanta, left her home and job and fled to Indigo Isle. What had she been doing here, besides playing farmerette, he wondered?

Certainly not waiting for her husband, who'd turned up dead on the Caribbean island of Santa Luisa. As for the half million dollars, it had turned up missing. And as for Ali, everyone had an angle. She was no exception.

WIPING THE PERSPIRATION that dripped from his face on his shirtsleeve, Sam had to admit he'd struck out in his first fact-finding expedition on Indigo. But that didn't matter because there was plan B.

Sam had learned two ways to work a case, outside or inside. Outside meant hours of tedious surveillance, hundreds of phone calls, frequent bribes to computer hackers and interview after interview with informants or anyone with information about the suspect.

An inside operation meant getting close to the suspect, knowing how he lived and felt, what went on in his head, sometimes even breathing the air he breathed. Working inside meant facing the enemy head-on and outsmarting him. Sam thought about the man who'd cleaned out his wealthy wife's bank account and headed west. Thanks to a trail of credit-card charges, Sam had found him in a plush Las Vegas hotel, bought him a few drinks, even gambled with him. They'd talked late into the night about the errant husband's unhappy marriage—before Sam had called the local police and turned him in.

That was working the inside. So was the Casey Bell-Ali Paxton case. He had proximity, he had an entrée—of sorts—and he had cover.

Now all he needed was an opportunity.

He wasn't sure whether Ali's looks were a help or hindrance. Entanglements with female clients—and occasionally suspects—happened. Sometimes there was no way to avoid them, but Sam made sure they were brief and never serious. He was used to being alone, and he liked his life the way it was. Being a private investigator allowed him to observe situations from afar, get involved when he was ready and then walk away when the time was right. Indigo Isle would be no different.

SAM TRUDGED ALONG under the relentless sun toward his cottage. He'd bought a few more staples for his kitchen even though he hated to cook. Here on Indigo Isle he had no choice.

He heard the honking of a horn and then a familiar voice. Not Ali, but her cousin Gwen.

"Hey, there, Sam. Get on in. I'll give you a ride back to the cottage. It's too hot for hiking."

A ride was more than welcome. He clambered into the truck.

Gwen wore a big straw hat that partially shielded her freckled face. She looked sideways at Sam under the brim. "In your condition this heat could wear you out. I'm surprised your wife didn't come along to look after you, and all."

"No wife," Sam replied emphatically. "I'm strictly solo. I thought you knew that."

"Why, no, I didn't," Gwen responded in her most sugary Southern accent, following with a solicitous question. "Are you on any kind of medication? When we take our son over to Charleston for his guitar lessons, we can pick up your prescriptions."

Sam knew she was fishing, and he knew why—curiosity about his need for a "rest cure" on Indigo Isle. "No," he said honestly, "I'm not taking any medicine. I was just stressed out at my job. Reorganization, pressure."

"I guess you just needed to get away."

She'd taken the hook. "Yeah. Eighty-hour weeks can be rough, especially in the insurance business."

Gwen seemed satisfied—and impressed—which was what Sam wanted. It wouldn't hurt for her and Tiger to think he was a top-notch respectable businessman, and certainly insurance was respectable. It was a career role he'd used before, and he thought he did it well. He hoped Tiger and Gwen would pass on their positive impressions to Ali.

Gwen was nodding. "Rough is right. That's why Tiger gave up his law practice to move back to the island.

'Course, now we're busier than ever. But it's a healthy kind of busy. We're enjoying it."

"I'd be interested in a tour of the facilities," Sam said eagerly. "All the spices and the . . ." He couldn't think of what else there'd be to see, but Gwen didn't seem to notice.

"We'll be pleased to arrange that. Maybe Ali can show you around."

There was a little gleam of mischief in Gwen's eyes as she pulled up in front of Sam's cottage. Matchmaking, Sam thought. That was all right with him. In fact, he couldn't ask for anything better.

"I'd like that. When?"

Gwen laughed. "Oh, soon." She cut her eyes toward him. "You aren't bored, are you, Sam?"

"No. Not at all. It's just tough to . . . to slow down all at once no matter what's prescribed. I'm the kind of guy who always needs to keep busy."

"Do you sail?"

"Well . . ." he equivocated.

"There's a little Sailfish under the porch of your cottage. It's just a flat board with sails attached, but it's fun in the water."

Sam climbed out of the truck. "Maybe I'll try it," he said politely.

Gwen rammed the truck into gear. "Be careful, though. We often have late-afternoon storms."

"Sure, I'll watch out for them."

"See you!"

Sam watched the receding truck, wondering what would happen if he went sailing down the shore in front of Ali's cottage. He certainly wasn't a sailor, so what if . . . ?

Whistling to himself, Sam walked toward the cottage.

"PUT HIGHFALUTIN TASTE in your low-country cookin'." Ali typed the words on her computer, looked up at the screen and hit the Delete key.

"Awful," she said to herself. She'd borrowed the laptop computer from the office and was working in her favorite spot—in front of the living room window with a view of the sea. The waves rushed in, seabirds flew upward as the tide drew back to reveal a smattering of tiny shells. Then the birds returned, scavenging quickly before the next wave.

Ali never tired of the pattern of tides that each late afternoon whipped up. They accompanied oncoming summer storms that either passed over or descended briefly on the island. She was so used to the storms she didn't pay any attention to them. There wasn't even any lightning today.

"'Spice up your life. . . .' No, that's too obvious," she muttered. "Need to tie in Christmas. Spices. Aromas. Holiday festivities . . ." She did some frantic brainstorming, but nothing clicked.

"How can anyone think of Christmas in July?" she grumbled. Christmas had become her least favorite holiday. In fact, it was her least favorite day of the year, and she wondered if she'd ever be in the mood for it again.

She took off her reading glasses and rubbed her temples, eyes closed. When she opened them and looked out across the beach to the sea, something caught her eye.

She stood and went to the window. There was a strange thrashing movement in the water. She reached for her binoculars, but before putting them to her eyes Ali knew what had happened. Sam Cantrell had invaded her life again.

"That idiot..."

Her neighbor was vainly struggling to right a small Sailfish that had overturned in the wind. Ali's lips curved into a smile. Even though the boat was lightweight, the sails were wet and heavy to maneuver, especially for someone who had no idea what he was doing. Clearly that was Sam. She watched him pull and push, trying to climb back aboard as the wind and waves enveloped him again.

Ali would have rushed to the rescue if the novice had been in any danger, but in fact he was waist-deep in the water and couldn't possibly have drowned—whether or not he managed to get back on the Sailfish. But there was a storm brewing, and that meant lightning, which could be dangerous.

With a sigh of resignation Ali kicked off her sandals, pushed open the screen door and ran down the steps and over the sand to the ocean's edge. Standing in the lapping water, she cupped her hands into a megaphone.

"Hey, Cantrell, come on in! A storm's brewing!"

Her words were blown away on the wind, and he appeared neither to hear nor see her.

"Oh, hell," she muttered and waded farther out. She jumped high to avoid the breaking waves and then finally, cursing, dived under the last big wave. Coming up, she saw the boat break loose from Sam's hold and shoot toward her, dangerous as a weapon. She dodged, reached out and grabbed the sail.

"This wasn't a very bright idea, Cantrell," she shouted.

"*Now* you tell me! I can't seem to get it upright."

She gave directions quickly. "Reach under the sail and push. I'll pull on this side."

Waves slapped at them as the wind intensified, but Ali kept pulling until they were knee-deep in the water. Then she moved around until she was on his side and could help him push. Their bodies were pressed together with Ali in front and Sam reaching over her. His chest was hard against her back; one of her legs was braced against his.

His arm grazed her breast as he reached for a rope, caught it and then lost it. A huge wave broke on top of them just as the lightning split the sky.

"Hold on!" she yelled as the boat started to skid away from them.

They grabbed together, missed and had finally managed to get a hold when another wave inundated them, picked up the boat, tossed it high and then shot it toward the shore.

There wasn't a chance that either of them could hold on. They lost their footing at the same time and were tossed about as haphazardly as the boat. The Sailfish soared over their heads and came to rest on the shore while Ali and Sam tumbled together in half a foot of water.

Lying breathless in the wet sand, Ali felt the strong sensation of hot flesh and hard muscles enveloping her. Sam Cantrell was lying on top of her! His legs were tangled with hers, his arms held her close. The weight of his chest pressed against her breasts. They were strangers who had suddenly become as intimate as lovers.

He looked down at her, a cocky smile on his face that was only inches from hers. "Thanks for the rescue, Ali. I guess I'm your catch of the day."

"My what?"

A mischievous delight lit up his eyes, and then his mouth was on hers. She couldn't avoid the salty taste of his lips and then she realized that she didn't want to.

He was kissing her, and she was kissing him back! For a wild irrational moment she let herself revel in the kiss, in the pure sensation of it—the pressure of his lips on hers, of their hearts pounding, bodies straining toward each other. A primitive excitement pulsed through Ali. She felt her body come alive with pleasure and awareness. And a sudden sharp longing. She opened her mouth under his kiss.

A wave washed over them, and Ali came up sputtering. She pushed Sam away and sat up. "You obviously know nothing about sailing." Her words were sharp, designed to wipe the self-satisfied smirk from his face and let him know the kiss meant nothing.

He grinned at her. "Not a damn thing."

"Then why did you take the Sailfish out in a storm?"

"There wasn't a storm at the time."

"Only black clouds all across the horizon," she lectured.

"I'm not a weatherman." He leaned toward her, and Ali thought he was going to try to kiss her again. His leg was still draped casually over hers, a long, lean, muscular leg. She rolled over and struggled to her feet.

"Not a weatherman...not a sailor...but you were on the sea in a storm."

"I wanted to get your attention." He stood beside her. The waves tugged at their feet.

"Well, you accomplished that. I should have let you flounder out there."

"What if I'd drowned? You would've been sorry."

"You weren't going to drown in four feet of water." She stalked toward the boat.

He followed. "Anything is possible with a novice like me."

"Next time we'll know better than to let a novice take out one of our boats."

She was all business now, as if the tussle in the waves and the kiss had never happened. She grabbed at the boat's bow. "Pull. We'll get it above the tide line, and you can stow it later."

He followed orders and then helped her drop the sails as the skies broke open with a heavy, drenching rain.

"Run for it," she shouted over the roar of the rain.

"We couldn't get much wetter," he called out to her. Sam's hair was plastered to his skull, and water dripped off his nose.

She looked back at him and in spite of herself suddenly began to laugh. "You do have a talent for getting wet, Sam Cantrell. Come on, I'll lend you a towel."

3

DRIPPING WET, Sam followed Ali up the stairs and into her cottage. She hadn't invited him in, but Sam didn't think she'd slam the door in his face. Outside, the rain fell in great gray sheets, blotting out sea and sky.

She opened a closet and tossed him a towel. "You can use that. I'm going to change."

Sam stood in the middle of the room, holding the towel and managing to bite back his words. He wanted to tell her to leave on her shorts and the T-shirt that was molded to her body like a second skin. It cupped her breasts and showed clearly the outline of her nipples. He could feel his muscles tightening with erotic tension, but she didn't seem to have a clue what she was doing to him, standing wet and glistening like a goddess from the sea. She must have felt something when they'd lain entangled in the waves and he'd kissed her with such intensity.

Get a grip, Cantrell, he warned himself. She reacted spontaneously to his kiss, and then she'd stalked away, acting as if it never happened. He should do the same. Sex and romance weren't part of the deal, but every time he was around Ali he became intensely aware of all the possibilities.

"Would you like some coffee? You can have it with sugar or without."

Sam grinned. He'd suspected all along she was on to his sugar scam. "How about a brandy—to take the chill off."

"Chill?" Her laughter was unexpected and thoroughly charming, that throaty sound that had appealed to him before. "It's ninety degrees outside."

"Remember, I'm convalescing. Sort of," he added.

She raised an unbelieving eyebrow. "So Gwen says. Okay, help yourself to brandy. It's in that cabinet next to the bookcase."

He watched her walk away, finding the view of her backside even more appealing than he'd expected. Take a good, long look, Sam, he told himself. You'll probably never get a chance to see Ali's bottom going away from you in wonderfully wet shorts again.

He stripped away his drenched T-shirt, tossed it on the porch and dried off. Draping the towel over his shoulder, he made his way across the room to the liquor cabinet, an antique, he noticed, like many of the pieces of furniture in the spacious, high-ceilinged room—so different from his cottage, which had been aptly named Flattop. Sam poured two brandies, left them on the cabinet and sank onto a canvas captain's chair, avoiding the inlaid wicker chairs with their comfortable cushions. Those old pieces of furniture, which he imagined were also handed down from her family, weren't the place to deposit his wet bottom.

Ali reappeared, decorously clothed in a heavy white terry-cloth robe. Her wet hair was slicked back from her face. He couldn't help staring. *Pretty* wasn't a word to describe Ali Paxton Bell. She was strong, vibrant, full of sexual energy. And more—passionate and unpredictable.

"Couldn't find the brandy?" Ignoring his stare and not giving him time to answer, Ali went to the cabinet, crouched down and found the bottle. With the movements, her robe gaped slightly to expose a tanned expanse of thigh and the flash of a curving breast. Sam held his breath and felt like a teenager. Unknowingly, Ali could make his every fantasy come to life.

She straightened, holding the bottle. "Here it is."

"Yeah, so it seems," he said innocently.

Standing, she saw the two filled glasses. "Oh. Why didn't you tell me?"

"You didn't give me a chance. Besides, I liked watching you bend over." Her look told him he shouldn't have said that.

She handed him a glass, which he immediately clicked against hers.

"To neighbors who come to the rescue."

"You were in no danger of drowning."

"Who knows." Sam took a swig of the drink. "There could have been strong undercurrents, ferocious sharks, deadly—"

"Deadly..."

"Jellyfish?"

She repeated the throaty laugh that Sam knew he could easily come to love.

"I've never been much of a water person. Guess I just need to be looked after, don't I?" He pulled a boyish face.

"Maybe so, but not by me. I'm far too busy at the computer today. So drink up, Sam."

Aware that as soon as he finished his brandy she'd usher him out, he tried sipping slowly. "I guess you couldn't be talked into taking a break for dinner."

"No way. Sorry. I told you this morning that I'm up to my ears in work."

"You're going to send me back into the rain?"

"Look outside, Sam. The rain has stopped, and the sun's breaking through. There might even be a rainbow. I think you'll be able to get home safely."

"I'm sure I will." He put down his glass, aware that he was being summarily dismissed—again. It was getting tiresome, and he was beginning to wonder how he'd ever break through her reserve and find out what her game was. Even if he managed to work in questions about her past, it was a certainty that Ali would get around them, much as she was getting around him.

She'd also finished her brandy, and seemed to be waiting.

"Well, thanks again for the rescue," he mouthed.

"No problem. Just part of the island service for wayward visitors."

"And thanks for the towel." He pulled it from his shoulders and passed it on to Ali.

That's when she saw the ugly, puckered indentation just below his collarbone. Her eyes widened, and then she looked away in embarrassment, ashamed to be caught staring.

The scar was jagged and white against his tanned skin. Sam saw her reaction. "Not a pretty sight," he said lightly.

"No. I mean, yes. I'm sorry," she finished lamely.

"Nothing to be sorry about. It happened a long time ago."

Ali avoided looking at the scar, focusing instead on Sam's face. It was impassive, but there was something in his icy green eyes that was part pain and part warning. She decided not to ask about the scar. Clutching the damp towel, she searched for something else to say.

Sam made it easy. "Guess I'll let you get back to work." He retrieved the wet T-shirt and stepped out into the now-sunny afternoon.

Ali turned and went back to her desk. She sat down thoughtfully, thinking about Sam when she'd meant to concentrate on the advertising campaign that was supposedly at the top of her agenda. Sam didn't belong anywhere near the top, but she'd experienced such a strange and absurd episode at the beach that she couldn't help analyzing it. First she'd wrestled with a sailboat and then with a supposed sailor. Real but not real. It was almost as if he'd staged the whole thing and she'd fallen right in with his plan.

Ali shook her head and chastised herself. She was off again, probably jumping to conclusions, seeing plots where none existed, getting skittish over nothing.

Gwen seemed quite taken with Sam, and Tiger thought he was a nice guy, but a sixth sense told Ali that he wasn't a nice guy at all. The scar, even though healed, was mean and nasty. She was far from being an expert, but it looked like a gunshot wound to her. Of course, there might be a simple, innocent explanation. On the other hand, the scar could mean what she'd suspected all along, that Sam Cantrell attracted danger.

Who was he and what was he doing on Indigo Isle? She was more confused than ever about Sam and her reactions to him. What could possibly have possessed her to return his kiss? she wondered. So he looked good in a bathing suit—great, as a matter of fact. So they'd rolled around in the waves. . . .

"Nothing but reflex," she announced to a sea gull perched on the porch railing outside her window. "Any woman would have done the same. It means nothing. Nothing."

The sea gull cocked his head and then flew away, leaving Ali looking out across the deserted beach.

Usually the peace and solitude soothed her, but today the view made her feel lonely, lost and a little sad.

There hadn't been a man in her life since Casey—over two long years. And even before he left their house in Atlanta he'd become so preoccupied with business that he'd begun to stay away from her bed. But just because she'd been alone so long was no reason for her to begin fantasizing over a stranger on the island.

With an angry gesture Ali pushed her glasses back on the bridge of her nose and tried to concentrate on the computer screen before her. She hated to feel sorry for herself, and even more, she hated to be vulnerable. Sam Cantrell was stirring up in her all kinds of feelings.

They'd surfaced when he'd kissed her on the beach, and Ali was afraid that they'd stay with her, disturbing, annoying feelings that weren't easy to avoid.

Ali watched the sea gull cautiously return to his perch, and tried to pretend that working at Spice of Life was enough in *her* life and that she was perfectly content on Indigo. Most of the time she succeeded. Being with Gwen, Tiger and Brian helped, but they had their own lives.

"What about mine?" she asked the bird.

She had come to realize that her life in Atlanta had been an extension of her husband's. Casey, by the force of his personality, had made his dreams hers. The big house, the high profile, the need for power and success. And she'd gone along with him because he was Casey Bell, who always got what he wanted. Her prestigious job had complemented him; her expensive car and designer clothes had reflected his success. And of course she had wanted to please him.

Ali's own dreams were much simpler than Casey's— work she could take pride in, a home, children and a man she could trust. Well, she had trusted Casey, and he'd smashed their marriage and their future. Now her instincts told her to stay alert, keep her defenses in place and guard her heart against Sam Cantrell.

Ali sat for half an hour, talking occasionally to the bird, staring at the screen, trying to think about her work. But it was hopeless. Instead of coming up with great advertising slogans she found that her head was filled with memories and, for the first time in years, uneasy stirrings of anticipation for what might come next.

JULY THIRD DAWNED much like the day before and the day before that on Indigo Isle—hot, sunny and steamy. There was one difference for Sam. He was in a worse mood than he'd been in since arriving on the island. He hadn't slept well at all, having spent half the night chasing a lizard around the house, into corners, up and down the walls, until he finally trapped it in an empty box and tossed it outdoors to join its extended lizard family. By then he was too wide-awake to do much more than lie on his bed listening to the wind in the palms and pines.

Sam was used to being by himself, but in this funny little cottage, listening to unfamiliar night sounds, he suddenly felt lonely. He wished he'd brought a television or radio to keep him company. He would even have liked an acquaintance to share a beer.

He kicked off the sheet and replayed the day's events in his mind. Ali's kitchen, warm and intimate in the morning sunlight. Tate Loomis's defense of Ali and the first family of Indigo. Gwen's suggestion about the sailboat and her sly smile when he'd said he was single— which she well knew.

At least she'd stopped at that and not asked why. He'd been asked that question a hundred times, and he knew all the right answers. He wasn't married because he never had found the right woman, didn't have enough time, wasn't ready to settle down. The usual litany.

But there was only one answer, and deep in his heart Sam knew it. He wasn't capable of intimacy, of opening himself up, of being vulnerable.

"You're a loner, Cantrell," he mumbled into the darkness. "That's why you're in this damned lumpy bed on this godforsaken island going stir crazy."

He sat up against the rickety headboard and looked out the window. Moonlight silhouetted Ali's cottage against the night sky. Was she sleeping? he wondered, or lying awake like him? He thought about her curled up in bed. He remembered her body and how it had felt against his, the smoothness of her thigh, the softness of her breast. Then he had a sudden memory that was even more disturbing, the way her mouth had opened under his. For a brief moment he'd felt her return his kiss, and then she'd changed into the abrupt, disdainful woman he'd met the first day.

Ali Paxton Bell. A riddle enclosed in an enigma. Could he break the code?

"You damned well better, Cantrell. It's your job," he chided himself. "That's what you're here for. So think about the case, not the kiss."

Finally, near dawn, he fell asleep, but it was a fitful sleep that ended when the sun streamed through the flimsy curtains and lit Flattop with the usual blinding light of morning on Indigo Isle.

He sat on the porch with his sugarless coffee and waited for Ali to leave. She obliged him right at nine o'clock, carrying the laptop computer and a sheaf of papers. He watched her go with an attitude, carefully orchestrated, of studied uninterest.

After a few minutes he walked over to her cottage, wearing shoes this time. He climbed the stairs, listening to the silence of the house and its surroundings. Then he knocked loudly on the front door.

"Ali, Ali, it's your neighbor. I need to borrow..."

Of course, there was no answer. His performance had been strictly for the sea gulls that whirled, screaming, above him.

Convinced that no one locked up on Indigo Isle, he pushed on the door. Not surprisingly, it swung open at his touch.

Sam had checked out the living room before, but now he sneaked a look into the nooks and crannies, quickly, expertly. He didn't expect to find the missing money taped to the back of a painting or tucked behind a sofa pillow. But surely there was something, somewhere, a clue as to how Casey had disposed of the money. So far, no accomplice had turned up, and Casey's wife remained the only suspect.

The living room revealed nothing except a box of computer disks on an antique desk by the window. Sam flipped through them expectantly, only to find them all clearly labeled as Spice of Life advertising and marketing plans.

He moved on to the bedroom, which was dominated by her four-poster bed. It was covered with an antique quilt, well washed and lovingly worn. Sam allowed his fingers to drift along the quilt, knowing it had no clues to offer him but somehow drawn to it. Ali had slept under it, curled up, her body warm and pliant.

The bedside table was crowded with family photos — Gwen, Tiger and a small boy, an older couple, possibly Ali's parents, both of whom had features that reflected in her stunning face. Casey Bell himself was significantly absent from the gallery.

As he moved around the room, and then became drawn back to her bed, Sam was tantalized by the scent of Ali's perfume. It hung in the air, and he drank it in thirstily. Then a fantasy slipped into his mind, unbidden. Holding on to the bedpost, he watched it unfold in vivid sensuality. He and Ali were on her bed, making love, enjoying every passionate moment, her long legs wrapped around his back, her mouth open, exploring.

Sam shook his head to rid himself of the image. Then, turning on his heel, he left her room. He was searching for facts, not fantasies, and her bedroom had offered nothing but a kind of dreamy lust that threw him off course, just exactly as Ali usually did.

The guest bedroom was next, and except for the packing boxes in the corner it offered very little in the way of clues. There was one possibility: the boxes could be filled with Casey's belongings, which Ali hadn't bothered to unpack. Sam was moving toward them when he heard a familiar noise. It was Ali's car.

Moving instinctively, quick as island lightning, he closed the space between him and the bedroom door, crossed the living room and stepped onto the front porch just as Ali opened the back door.

Avoiding the path to Flattop, he headed in the opposite direction, took cover in a stand of pine trees at the edge of the beach and waited. She'd left with her computer, all set to go to work. What the hell was she doing home?

Before Sam had a chance to answer his question, Ali reappeared, carrying the box of disks, which she'd obviously forgotten. Sam watched her drive off, and then got his second surprise of the day. She drove straight to Flattop, stopped and got out of the car. When she didn't get an answer to her knock, she scribbled a note and left it in the screen door.

He'd been all set to go back to his sleuthing when she left, but curiosity got the best of him, and he went straight to his own cottage and retrieved the note.

Sam, we're having a Fourth of July picnic tomorrow at the big house. Tiger and Gwen want you to join us. How about five o'clock?

Sam smiled to himself as he pocketed the note, but not before noticing that it had originally read: I want you to join us. She'd scratched out the "I" and replaced it with "Tiger and Gwen." She'd been flustered—a good sign.

He was smiling as he went into the cottage, prepared to face another scorcher followed by a boring, lonely evening of no TV and canned ravioli. Never mind. The Fourth of July was only a day away. And he expected fireworks all around.

"THE FIREWORKS WILL COME later," Ali explained to Sam as they took their glasses of lemonade out onto the big house veranda.

"Oh?" Sam lifted an eyebrow and smiled devilishly.

Ali ignored the inference. "Yes, they set them off a couple of miles down the beach. We have a great view from here."

"I'm looking forward to that," Sam said.

Ali cut her eyes toward him, doubting his seriousness but not unaware of something else that seemed to happen every time they made eye contact. She cursed herself for getting caught with him in the ocean two days earlier, for rolling over and over in the waves and then letting him kiss her.

"Ali—"

Before he could speak, a boy's voice called out from the lawn. Brian raced toward them with the dogs on his heels. "Look what I found," he yelled. "It's definitely an Indian arrowhead." He held out a triangular stone for Sam to examine.

Sam turned it over carefully. "Looks like it could have been on the end of an arrow to me."

"Do you know anything about Indian arrowheads?" Ali asked.

Sam laughed and gave the stone back to Brian. "Not the slightest thing, but I'm willing to learn."

"Then come on in my room. I'll show you my collection," Brian offered.

"Sam, you don't have to—"

"Nonsense, Ali, I'm a great fan of enthusiasts like Brian," he said as he followed the boy into the house, passing Gwen on the way.

"Where're they going?" Gwen asked after she'd settled into a chair beside Ali.

"Guess."

"To see Brian's collections?"

Ali nodded.

"Don't you think we should attempt to rescue him?"

"Nope, one rescue is enough."

Gwen looked puzzled, but Ali decided not to clue her in. "Sam's been looking for entertainment during his stay on the island. Now he has it," she said wickedly.

"You're enjoying his torment, Ali!"

"Maybe."

Gwen sipped her lemonade. "And are you also enjoying *him?*"

"What are you talking about?"

"I don't mean his body or—"

"Gwen!"

"I mean *him*, his personality and all."

"I've seen Sam a couple of times since he moved into Flattop. That's all. I know absolutely nothing about his body—I mean, his personality."

Gwen laughed but Ali didn't join in.

"I'm not that easily seduced."

"Too bad," Gwen said in an aside.

"As I was saying, I'm not as easily taken in as you and Tiger. The man has a dark side." She didn't mention the scar. Somehow that would seem a betrayal of confidence though she wasn't sure that she owed anything to Sam.

"When did you see him?" Gwen persisted.

"Oh, he staged some fake meetings. He came over to borrow sugar, and then he pretended to lose control of the Sailfish." Ali smiled. "Actually, he *did* lose control, and I ran out to rescue him, kind of."

"Obviously he wants to get to know you, and that's very flattering. You two are young, attractive, healthy. Why shouldn't you have some fun together?"

"The meetings seemed so . . . so contrived," Ali muttered.

"Oh, Ali!" Gwen threw up her hands in disgust. In the moist heat of the afternoon her red hair curled around her face and her freckles seemed more prominent than ever. "You're determined to see shadows where none exist. Has he done anything suspicious except to pursue you?"

"Well . . . no."

"I rest my case," Gwen pronounced.

Before Ali could respond a resounding crash came from the kitchen.

"I wonder if that's my cue to help Tiger?" Gwen asked, unexcited, still sipping away at her lemonade.

"Sounds pretty urgent."

"Hmm." Gwen didn't move.

"What do you suppose he's doing?"

"Putting the little pot in the big one, as his mamma used to say, concocting something special to show off for our guest."

"Well, he's certainly doing it with gusto."

"You know Tiger. Nothing halfway." Gwen pushed back her chair. "If I help him with dinner, will you promise to rescue Sam one more time?"

"Oh, all right," Ali agreed.

"And honey, be nice. After all, he *is* company. Southern hospitality and all that," she called over her shoulder.

SAM AND BRIAN WERE side by side on Brian's bed, poring over a book of some kind, the two panting dogs lolling at their feet.

Ali imagined Brian had brought out not only his Indian arrowheads but his baseball cards and seashells. She thought of joining them and then decided to give Brian a chance to have Sam to himself for a while longer.

Brian was describing his treasures in minute detail with Sam getting in an occasional question. He had a way with kids, Ali admitted to herself grudgingly. Brian really seemed to like him. Charmed by the scene, she strolled closer to the door and listened.

"Ali gave me most of these stamps," Brian was explaining. "She used to collect them when she was a kid."

"They're very nice," Sam replied. "There sure are a lot of them."

Ali smiled as she sensed the despairing resignation in Sam's voice.

"You don't have to look at every one, not tonight, anyway," Brian reassured him. "Just these—some of my newest stamps, and my best."

"Yeah, I see. You're a lucky kid. I never had much of a chance to collect anything when I was young."

"You could always start now," Brian told him seriously.

Ali smiled again, this time more tenderly. She could hear the pages of the book turning as Brian kept up his running commentary.

"Here're some great new ones," Brian announced. "Mostly birds and butterflies, but there're some funny-looking people, too. Ali says they're a king and queen—"

Before he finished the sentence Ali was through the door in an instant. "Brian, I think Sam needs a break—and a drink. How about it, Sam?"

Sam flashed her a look of unadulterated gratitude.

"You haven't shown him your new camera, Brian. It's out on the front porch. You might even want to take some pictures of our picnic."

"Great idea, Ali. I'll see you outside!" He clattered out of the room, stamps forgotten. The dogs raced behind, sliding on the hardwood floors.

Ali slipped the book back into its place on the shelf. "Tiger's almost ready to start the picnic. I'm sorry Brian monopolized you so long."

"It's okay. Anything to ingratiate myself with you. Did I succeed?" he teased.

Ali smiled despite herself. She was beginning to think Gwen was right. Sam wasn't a threat. All he wanted was a little summer romance.

"You never give up, do you?"

He followed her along the hall. "Not now. Not ever."

THE PARTY TOOK PLACE in a gazebo at the bay's edge, a Victorian-looking building screened against the ever-present evening mosquitoes. Ali sat across the table from Sam, who happily enjoyed his view of her in blue shorts and a red-and-white-striped shirt worn in honor of the Fourth. Gwen sat next to Sam, and Tiger took his place at the head of the picnic table, although he didn't do much sitting. He was up and down, constantly replenishing the serving dishes and insisting Sam have one more helping.

Brian ate quickly and disappeared with his camera, his dogs and his friends while the adults leisurely enjoyed the meal. Sam was full of praise for Tiger's cooking, and his host was more than willing to share his knowledge of coastal South Carolina cuisine.

"My mamma taught me all about low-country cooking when I was just a little fella. 'Course, my wife has taught me all about plants and herbs."

Gwen beamed under his praise.

Crayfish gumbo was served piping hot, poured onto bowls of fluffy white rice. "No one around here would say crayfish, by the way," he observed. "It's crawfish."

"However it's pronounced, I'm all for it," Sam said, taking another big bite.

"I like a man with a good appetite. Sometimes these women let me down because they won't eat enough," Tiger observed.

"Let you down?" Ali challenged. "We sample recipes all day long—"

"Until we can't hold one more bite," Gwen finished. "But it's nice to have a new guinea pig, Sam."

"Happy to oblige. Could a noncook like me turn out a meal like this if I bought your spice mixes?"

"Sure," said Tiger.

"Not a chance," Ali replied at the same time.

"You see the difference between the optimist and the pessimist in the family," Gwen said. "The real answer to your question is yes and no. Yes, you can buy the spices, but no, you can't turn out a meal like this—"

"I told you," Ali interrupted.

"Unless you buy the shrimp boil mix and a pound of jumbo shrimp. Then all you have to do is stir." She sat back with a satisfied smile.

"It takes a little more talent than that," Ali attempted.

"No, it doesn't," Gwen argued.

But Sam was already laughing. "Even I can do it, Ali," he said, giving her foot a little nudge.

Sam's nudge was friendly, Ali thought, neighborly, and there was mischievous invitation in his eyes. Lulled by Sam's camaraderie with her family and intrigued by his easy charm, Ali felt her defenses eroding. After all, this *was* a holiday and everyone was having fun. She decided to join in.

"Since I'm in charge of sales and marketing, I'll be happy to ply you with a gross of everything. We take checks or credit cards—if you have the proper ID."

There was a gleam in her eye, and this time Sam knew she was joking. Something had subtly changed since he'd arrived at the Mallorys' for the Fourth of July celebration. Ali was a little friendlier and definitely less suspicious, although still standoffish. Maybe that would change, too.

IT WAS THE LANGUOROUS time of day, between light and dark, when a soft breeze wafted from the ocean as the frogs and crickets began their evening serenade. The four adults pushed back their chairs and got comfortable, finishing up a second bottle of wine. From somewhere nearby came the sounds of children mimicking exploding fireworks.

"The great collector," Tiger said. "Brian also has a variety of noises, which he's taught all his friends. This is the fireworks collection."

"And his parents have a spice collection," Sam observed, "which they grow in their own greenhouses."

Tiger laughed. "I can tell you aren't a cook, son. We grow *herbs* here—basil and thyme, rosemary, marjoram and sage. Even some of the old-timey ones such as sorrel and hyssop, just like in the nineteenth century."

Sam savored the sound of the names. He'd never heard of sorrel or hyssop.

"But we don't grow spices," Tiger went on. "We import those from all around the world, mix them with our herbs in our workrooms—"

"According to *our* recipes," Gwen added.

"And ship them out."

Ali's long legs were propped on a low stool; her hair was pulled up on her head, and a few tendrils escaped, curling around her face. She looked relaxed and content. Her shapely fingers played with the stem of the wineglass. She grinned conspiratorially at Sam. "I'll let you in on a high-level marketing discovery. 'Herb of Life' didn't catch on with the customers."

"But we all need some *spice* in our lives, don't we?" Gwen piped in.

Sam wondered what kind of message Gwen was sending. He had a feeling that she was aiding and abetting his pursuit of Ali. For a brief moment he felt guilty of misrepresenting himself to the Mallorys, whom he liked immensely. Then he shrugged off the feeling. What he was doing was for everyone's good in the long run.

"You folks are quite a team." They were, he thought— close, loyal, supportive and protective.

"We take care of each other," Tiger said.

"No spice spies allowed." Ali grinned at Sam, and he flashed her a smile. Things were going well now, smooth and comfortable, just the way he wanted.

"Then I guess you won't tell me what was in that shrimp boil?"

"Oh, I'll tell you," Tiger said magnanimously. "Actually, the ingredients are on our label. It's the proportions that no one knows, and with these recipes there's nothing as disastrous as guesswork. Each amount is carefully balanced. Those Carolina shrimp were boiled in a mix of peppercorns and bay leaves, red pepper flakes, coriander—"

"Wow!" Sam said. "No wonder my taste buds sat up and took notice."

"There's more. We don't cheat our customers. Celery seed, salt, ginger and mace—"

"Mace?" Sam was startled.

"Not the kind you spray on an attacker," Gwen answered. "Mace is a sort of spice. Comes from the same tree as nutmeg. It grows somewhere in the Caribbean. Windward Islands, I think."

Sam looked at Gwen and tried to keep his face impassive. "Windward Islands?"

"I believe so. Isn't that it, Tiger?"

Before her cousin had a chance to answer, Ali suddenly stood. "Come on, let's help Tiger organize all these dishes and make room for dessert. Homemade peach ice cream, eh, Tiger?"

Sam got up with the others and began to stack dishes, hardly listening to the talk around him. The Mallorys had dealings with the Windward Islands. Was it simply a coincidence that Casey Bell's body had been found on Santa Luisa, right in the heart of the Windwards? He shelved that thought, adding it to his Ali research. This was his first breakthrough on Indigo.

4

ALI WAS FULL OF SURPRISES. And Sam, who considered himself pretty good at figuring people out, couldn't get a handle on her. From the beginning she hadn't been what he expected. Tonight was no exception.

Just when darkness settled around the gazebo like a black velvet curtain blotting out the pearl gray evening sky, her mood seemed to change. Or was it something that Gwen said?

The conversation had turned to the next Spice of Life campaign, the big push for Christmas that would begin with a booth at the Trade Mart in Atlanta in late July. Sam had commented that July seemed a little early to be thinking about Christmas. Then, at some point during Gwen's long explanation, Ali had abruptly excused herself to go for a walk on the beach. After a few polite moments Sam followed, promising to bring her back in time for the fireworks.

He caught up with her at the water's edge. "You almost lost me in the dark. Was that the point?"

"Not at all," she answered. "I really wanted to lose Gwen and Tiger—for a while, at least."

He walked along beside her. "Why's that?"

"Oh, it's the Christmas thing. They've been pushing me to go with them to Atlanta when the Spice of Life booth opens at the mart."

"Seems logical. You're the marketing arm of the company. I don't know much about merchandising, but I gather from Gwen that retail shops do their buying for the Christmas season in July, right?"

"Right. And this'll be our first booth at the mart, so it's a quantum leap into the big time."

"Then they'll need you, right?"

"Wrong. I operate from here. The brochures and ad copy are in the works. Everything'll be ready for the opening. Then it's up to them. Tiger'll do the cooking demonstrations, and Gwen can take orders."

"Doesn't someone have to hand out the samples, talk to the customers, handle the press?"

"I avoid personal contact with the press whenever possible," was Ali's response.

Sam's shoes were filling with sand, and he stopped to take them off and roll up his pant legs. Ali was already barefoot, carrying her sandals.

"Doesn't that sort of defeat the purpose?" he asked.

"Taking off your shoes or rolling up your pants?" she responded.

She sure was good at skirting issues, Sam thought. "Avoiding the press."

"They get our PR packets. I just don't deal with them personally."

"Fair enough. I didn't come out here to talk about the press, anyway."

"Neither did I." Her reply was adamant.

"Why *did* you come?"

"Besides to get away from my persistent cousins? To cool off, enjoy the beach. This is my favorite time."

The moon was rising over the sea, lighting a glittering path along the tide line. The breeze was tangy with the scent of the salty night air. Ali looked up at Sam as he walked beside her. Gwen was right about one thing. He was handsome, especially when the moonlight lent a silvery sheen to his dark hair and delineated the strong planes of his face. She quickly looked away and got her mind back on the subject at hand. "Thanks for not pressuring me about the Trade Mart thing."

"It's your decision."

"I know, but every time the subject comes up, Gwen and Tiger jump on me. The problem is, I know they're right. It would be helpful if I went with them, but I hate the thought of it."

"I can understand that. The traffic alone can be murder in Atlanta."

"It's not just Atlanta, although the thought of going back there gives me pause, too."

They'd reached a jetty, and Sam brushed the sand off a big rock, waited for Ali to settle back and then sat beside her.

"It's really Christmas that bothers me," she said. "I hate the holiday. It's hard enough to deal with here, but to be at the Trade Mart around all that fake merriment and false cheer—I can't do it." She realized that she'd spoken much more vehemently than she meant to. "You probably think I'm crazy."

The calmness of his answer surprised her. "It's an overproduced holiday, isn't it? So much hoopla and fanfare. So much commercialism. I can see why you'd be turned off."

"I can't believe you're on my side about it. Everyone else seems shocked that I have such negative feelings."

"I'm not everyone else," he said quietly. His eyes didn't leave hers, and Ali could see his expression perfectly in the light of the moon. He didn't touch her but his words were like a caress. They sent a little shiver down her spine. No, he wasn't like anyone else, not like anyone she'd ever known.

"I'm also not easily shocked by anything," he told her.

"And you don't like Christmas, either?"

"No. It was never a good time for me, especially when I was growing up. My dad was an alcoholic, so Christmastime was an excuse to drink even more, and of course my mom tried to get him to stop. It wasn't exactly a time of joy and family togetherness. He drank, she yelled and I spent most of the holiday season hiding out in the garage."

"I'm sorry."

He shrugged. "It was a long time ago. Life goes on, and we all grow up. But I never did learn to like Christmas, I guess because of all the bad associations. The worst one was my mom's illness. She was sick for a long time, and she died right before Christmas. I can't think of it with pleasure, so I try to ignore it. Christmas is just another day. I've spent it in bars and resorts and other people's homes—"

"Never had a Christmas tree of your own? Never hung stockings?"

"Never. Does that make me the Christmas grinch?"

"Not at all. It's just unusual."

"But you don't like the holidays, either," he reminded her.

"Not now, but when I was a child it was different." Her voice took on a wistful, nostalgic note. "When I was growing up, Christmas was a wonderful time of year."

"Tell me about it."

Ali felt a little funny sharing warm memories with someone whose childhood was so unhappy, but Sam insisted.

"My dad and I cut down the tree ourselves, and we all decorated it together," she remembered. "I made many of the ornaments with my mom, and we used them year after year. We didn't have much money, but my parents took pains to make sure everything about Christmas was special. Love and care shone in everything they did. Even after they died and Casey and I were married, I thought Christmas always would be that way. But maybe you have the right idea—no expectations of Christmas so no disappointments. I guess I was just the opposite. Too many damned expectations."

Sam heard the bright brittle edge in her voice. He thought of backing off and then changed his mind. "Is that what happened to you—a Christmas disappointment, expectations dashed?"

"Every last one of them."

Instinct told him to be quiet. If she was going to talk, it would be now. He'd been waiting for this, to hear it from her.

"Christmas two years ago turned into the worst day of my life, the day my husband left me and I found out he'd stolen half a million dollars. You probably read about Casey Bell's embezzlements. It was all over the papers."

He had to make a decision to lie or tell a half-truth. He opted for the second choice. "The name is familiar. I might have heard something."

"Everyone else in the world heard everything, it seems." Her voice was bitter. "My ex-husband removed half a million dollars from investment accounts he managed. Then he took off for the Caribbean and left me with a house full of presents, a Christmas tree, stockings hung on the mantelpiece of our new house—I never did think we could afford it, and I was right. We also couldn't afford the two Mercedes or the club membership, but Casey was so sure he'd make it big."

Ali was amazed at herself. She'd blurted everything out to Sam in half a dozen sentences, the whole episode of Casey Bell, golden boy, wheeler-dealer, hot young broker on his way up.

But as Sam had said, nothing shocked him. "So you were left holding the bag?"

"You bet. The police, lawyers, FBI and Federal Trade Commission, and anyone else you can think of, came after me as if I'd committed a crime. The press hounded me to death."

"So that's where you get your reluctance to face reporters. And you thought I was a reporter when I came to the island."

"They've tried to slip onto Indigo before, just for one more interview. Obviously if I knew anything I would have told the police, not the press, but they've never managed to figure that one out."

Sam waited a while and then slid into his next comment thoughtfully, nice and easy. "So Casey took off, and you took the heat. Hell, I'd be mad, too."

"I still am," she admitted.

"What about Casey?"

"He's . . . he—died."

Sam watched her carefully.

"He drowned in the Caribbean, just off an island called Santa Luisa. That's where he fled to, and I'm told he was planning to leave there for another place where he couldn't be extradited. Then there was the accident. He was alone, swimming by himself, and the riptide got him. It's ironic, isn't it?"

Sam nodded. "And no one knows what happened to the money." It was more a comment than a question.

She looked up sharply. "So you did read the papers?"

"It seems logical that if the money had been found, you wouldn't be hiding away here."

"I'm not hiding." Her voice was defensive. "I enjoy it here. It's quiet and peaceful. I love my work. I adore living on Indigo."

Silently Sam urged her to go on; in fact, he even nudged her a little with his elbow.

"Okay, okay. I protest too much, but it isn't bad here, and I'm very grateful to Tiger and Gwen for taking me in."

"And that's why you feel so guilty about not going to the Trade Mart even though it brings back awful memories of Casey, the money and Christmas."

Their arms were still touching. Ali didn't move away. "Gwen says I need to face the past and fight my dragons head-on."

"Remember, Ali, advice is cheap, and you get what you pay for."

Her lips curved in a smile.

The smile encouraged Sam to take her hand, which was already touching his. It felt warm and soft. She didn't pull away.

"So now it's *my* turn to give some advice."

Ali's laugh was musical; he loved to hear the sound. "Cheap advice?" she asked. But her expression was interested.

"Yep. You buying?"

They were still holding hands, and Ali let herself enjoy the moment, the touch of him, the excitement he generated. Then she replied as steadily as possible. "Try me."

"If I were you, I'd do just exactly what I wanted to. You can't manufacture enthusiasm about Christmas any more than I can, so don't try."

"Thanks, I don't plan to," Ali said.

"Besides," he added, studying her through narrowed eyes, "I can't see you handing out gumbo samples in the middle of July dressed in a reindeer outfit."

That brought more laughter. "I doubt if we'd wear costumes, although . . ."

"Although?" He gave her hand a squeeze.

"It might not be a bad idea," she answered slowly. "Oh, probably not a reindeer outfit, but maybe . . . a crawfish with a stocking cap."

"Or a shrimp on ice skates?"

"A skating crab would be better. More balance . . . eight legs, you know." She pursed her lips, thinking. "Not a bad image for our brochure. I have a great art director over in Charleston. I can fax her my ideas—"

"You're kidding."

"I'm not! You've inspired me, Sam. I've been stuck for a hook for the Christmas brochure. This could be it." She squeezed his hand, and Sam felt an almost childish glow of pleasure.

"I don't think I've ever been an inspiration to anyone."

"Well, you are for me tonight. You've let me get out my anger about Casey and you never once told me what I *should* do."

"Life is filled with too many shoulds." He pulled her to her feet, still holding her hand. "Come on, let's look for those fireworks."

As THE COLORS EXPLODED above them, green and blue and red against the black sky, Sam suddenly remembered. "I told your cousins we'd join them for this."

Ali watched a trail of gold and silver sputter out and fall from the sky. "Then I guess we'd better go back."

"Really?"

"Well . . ."

"Do you think they'll miss us?"

"Probably not. I expect Brian's asleep on the floor of the gazebo with his dogs curled around him."

"And Tiger?"

"He's cleared away the dishes and gone back to the big house. Pretty soon Gwen will put Brian to bed and then curl up with her favorite romance novel."

"Well, what a relief. We have the fireworks all to ourselves."

Just then a triple explosion illuminated the sky, beginning slowly with a wheel of green that suddenly erupted into a yellow fountain and then turned purple as it dropped into the sea.

The colors lit Ali's face as she tilted back her head to watch. "Isn't it great? Now this is a holiday I can get into. All these . . ."

"Explosions?" Sam asked innocently. The word had a sudden double meaning.

"Well, yes. Noise and light and— Oh, look!"

Together they stood and watched as the stars and stripes of the American flag exploded red, white and blue across the sky.

"I guess that's it," Ali said. "The fireworks here on Indigo are pretty limited."

"I think they're extraordinary."

"Extraordinary?" Ali cocked her head to the side, not understanding. The breeze blew a wisp of hair across her lips. Sam brushed it aside with his fingers, felt the smoothness of her skin, the softness of her hair.

They were standing close to each other. So close he could feel the warmth from her body and smell the scent of her perfume. He cupped her face with his hands and leaned toward her. His heart was pounding, as if he were a schoolboy. "And the fireworks are only the beginning," he whispered.

His lips grazed hers. Ali's were warm and soft, tasting of wine. He slid his arms around her waist and drew her close. There was a sudden recall—his body against hers in the wave, and then an anticipation of new, unexplored delights. Those delights were his now as her breasts, hipbone, thighs pushed against him. When her arms tightened slowly, tentatively around his neck, Sam felt a thrill of triumph and pleasure.

He kept his lips against hers, not breaking the pressure, tightening it, letting his breath mingle with hers. The warm summer air, the breezes, the waves lapping the shore, none of that made an impression on Sam. He could have been anywhere, any time, but he couldn't have been with anyone but Ali. She was sizzling in his arms.

As Sam moved his hand under her shirt, up the smooth, silky column of her back, he made a delightful discovery. Ali wasn't wearing a bra! He was surprised by that even though nothing about her should have surprised him by now. She made a little moaning sound, and he knew she'd felt his surprise.

For an instant he thought she would pull away. In fact, she tried to, but he held her more closely, knowing she wasn't trying all that hard. He deepened the kiss.

Slowly Ali's mouth opened under his, and Sam felt all the night's fireworks tingle along his spine and spread throughout his taut body.

Ali ran her fingers along Sam's neck and through the crisp texture of his hair. When she'd meant to push away from him, somehow she moved closer, molding her body more tightly against his big muscular frame.

Ali knew she should get away from whatever was happening. Should. Her world was full of shoulds. She was tired of them. So she *shouldn't* have been kissing Sam Cantrell on a moonlit Fourth of July. Never mind, her body told her calculating mind. The whole experience was very, very pleasurable.

Extremely so.

His mouth was warm and moist on hers, and when she opened her lips Ali felt the probing of his tongue. It was hotter and more demanding than the hot night, and it made her head spin, her bones and sinews and every fiber of her being sing out.

Ali drew a deep, convulsive breath and let her tongue touch his. A spiral of pleasure blossomed inside, its fragrance enriching her, its taste making her breathless. Her skin was on fire, and she begged him with her body not to stop.

He answered with his own body, still kissing her, exploring her mouth with his tongue, touching, teasing, tantalizing the silky recesses of her deep moistness. His body was tight all along hers. He shifted his bare feet in the sand, and she felt the hardness of his manhood against her.

He slid one hand to her buttocks, pulled them upward, pressing her close. Ali didn't resist that. She let her body mold to his while his other hand drifted to her back, under her arm, to the soft rise of her breast.

Her nipples were hard and taut with desire, tender as they rubbed the cotton of his shirt. For a wild moment she lost herself in the feeling of his hands, one under her bottom, the other pressing against her spine. She felt them both, separately but with equal intensity.

Then she took the thought even farther and added her imagination. She imagined his mouth moving from hers downward, downward to her breast. Those were wild, erotic ideas that she'd been holding at bay, dangerous ones that she shouldn't be thinking. Suddenly she knew that and tried, really tried this time, to break away.

"No—wait!" She twisted and turned until he let her go. But she didn't move back; instead she gave a deep sigh and rested her head against his chest, eyes closed. Her breathing was fast and irregular, and she willed herself to be calm. But the thudding in her heart refused to slow. It was as rapid as her thoughts and her visions, and yet it was no more rapid than his own heartbeat against her breast. She knew that Sam was as carried away by the kiss as she.

Ali raised her eyes to his. They were dark with passion and with a look so intent it sent a chill rippling along her spine. But his voice was low and sexy.

"See what I mean about fireworks, Ali?"

Her laughter was high-pitched, not natural sounding at all. It embarrassed her, but she tried to cover it with her response. "Yes. Umm, that was quite a surprise. I mean, I usually don't . . . I didn't mean to give you the wrong idea." That wasn't exactly what she'd meant to say, and it didn't help that she was still leaning against the warm column of his body. She stepped back, almost tripped, and he reached out to steady her.

"I don't have the wrong idea at all," he said slowly. "It was just a kiss, Ali, a kiss on a moonlight night." His lips curved in a smile. "I'm not going to say I'm sorry, though, because I'm not."

"Me neither." She was relieved to find that her voice was steady now, her breathing easier. "I mean, it was quite nice."

"Nice? That's it? I'm not sure that's much of a recommendation," he commented with another smile.

She was comforted by the joke. "Well, it was more than nice, but—"

"I know. Let's not get carried away by the moonlight and fireworks, huh?" He anticipated her with the next comment, a little sarcastic but on the mark. "I imagine you'll be real busy the next few days. Too busy to see me."

"Yes, I probably will be—busy with the Spice of Life brochure. The Christmas sea creatures and..." She carefully took a step backward, and he made no attempt to hold her.

"On ice skates," he said.

"Yes, and thanks again, I mean for the idea," she replied. "The brochure and all." Things between them seemed to be getting awkward again.

"You're welcome. May I walk you home?"

"No, I'd like to be alone for a while."

"But it's on my way, Ali."

"Please let me go ahead. I'll be safe," she said quickly. Gradually she'd been moving away from him, afraid of what had almost happened. It didn't take a great leap of imagination to get from envisioning what it would be like to feel Sam's tongue and mouth on her breasts to allowing it to happen. There was a safe distance between them now, and it was emotional as well as physical. She breathed a deep sigh. Everything had happened too fast. Sam was right; his kisses had set off fireworks inside her. Now the fireworks in the sky were over. She had no idea how to handle the fireworks inside.

He stood looking at her, saying nothing, and Ali fought down an impossible urge to walk toward him instead of walking away. It wasn't like her to get so involved with a stranger.

"Good night, Sam," she said, turning quickly before she lost her resolve. His own good-night followed her as she began running down the beach.

Sam watched her run, aching to run after her, hold her close, kiss her again—and make love to her this time.

He almost did just that. But something stopped him in his tracks. It wasn't in the plan. "The plan, you fool," he said aloud. The plan was to find out if she knew about the money and, if so, to recover it. That was his job. But then there was Ali, a different Ali from the one he had expected. She turned his plan around.

Sam stuffed his hands into his pockets and began walking back down the beach. Something had to happen soon. He had to find some leads or get the hell out of here. He couldn't take much more being so close to Ali.

He walked along, retracing their footprints in the sand, remembering the scene they'd just been through. After that, how could he believe she was guilty of anything except falling in love with the wrong guy? Or was it that he wanted her so much he was willing to believe her innocence?

Sam kicked at a wave that lapped around his feet. Most of the time he saw the world in shades of black and white. But Ali . . . she blurred all the lines. She was getting to him, and he couldn't do a damned thing about it.

There was one thing he could do, though, one thing he ought to do. Go to her and make a clean breast of it all, tell her who he was and why he was on the island. Maybe he just didn't have the guts to do that. Or maybe he still believed she was into this crime up to her ears.

Sam smiled to himself. She had lovely ears, small and set close to her head, with tendrils of her tousled hair curling around them. Suddenly he stopped in the sand.

He'd been thinking about his attraction to Ali, but suppose she wasn't attracted to him, suppose all of his fantasies would come to nothing, no matter what happened, no matter her guilt or innocence?

Then he remembered their kiss. Her reaction had been as intense as his own. He wasn't imagining it; they were attracted to each other, and something was going to happen if he didn't get to the bottom of the Casey Bell crime soon.

Stopping again, Sam realized that he'd gone past the beginning footprints in the sand. He looked toward the shore and couldn't recognize any landmarks. A top detective hot on the trail of a mystery, and he was lost on the beach at Indigo Isle!

JULY FIFTH DAWNED as hot as the Independence Day before—cloudless blue sky, debilitating humidity and total lack of breeze. Sam was getting tired of the sameness of the days, which were bad enough at Flattop but were really murder inside the one phone booth on Indigo Isle.

It was next to the Loomis store, and except for a small circle of shade thrown by the fronds of a scraggly palmetto tree, the booth was unprotected in the baking sun.

"Hot as twelve yards of hell, Jerry. At least, that's what my friend Tate Loomis told me this morning. Yes, Loomis. Oh, never mind. Tate's just another one of the island characters, and I couldn't begin to explain him to you. So just tell me what's happening at the office."

Sam squinted his eyes against the noon sun and listened intently to his partner.

"Yeah, I know the client's anxious, but I've only been here four days. I'm good, but I'm not a miracle worker."

Sam held the receiver away from his ear as Jerry Greenfield's voice rasped on the line. He waited an appropriate amount of time and then responded. "You don't have to tell me the obvious, Jerry. I'd like a break, too, but it's tougher than either of us could have imagined. I'm just beginning to make inroads with the family."

Sam listened to Jerry's response and then jumped in. "Listen, pal, these aren't the kind of people who are going to let a stranger in on their family secrets in one afternoon. You may live in Atlanta, but you're not a Southerner no matter how long you've been in this part of the world. And you sure aren't an islander. They're a different breed altogether."

Out of the corner of his eye Sam saw Tate Loomis step out on the porch of his store. Sam gave him a wave and then spoke more quietly into the receiver. "Listen, Jerry, I have one bit of information I want you to follow up. Got a pencil?"

Sam waited, still watching Loomis.

"Okay, ready? The island of Santa Luisa, where Bell was found, is in the Windwards. W-i-n...oh, hell, check the atlas. It's a string of islands between Guadeloupe and Grenada. Ali's family does business with spice companies down there. I know it's a hell of a long shot, but they must have pretty good connections. What if they're business partners, even friends, with someone in Santa Luisa, someone Casey trusted enough to give the loot to for safekeeping? That's my wild shot for now. I'm tossing it out to you. You're a detective, partner, so detect. Find out if anyone on Santa Luisa sells mace—no, not that kind of mace. It's a spice like nutmeg. Find out if anyone sells it to the Spice of Life company."

He waited for Jerry to stop sputtering and then went on. "How big can the island be? A few phone calls should give you what you need. If anyone knows Ali or her cousins, Thomas or Gwen Mallory, maybe we have a connection that will eventually lead us to where the dough is stashed."

Sam listened as Jerry repeated the instructions back to him. "Okay, that's it. I'll call when I get a chance. I didn't know the place was so damned primitive. Yes, I understand that, buddy. I'm being well paid, and I'll get even more if I turn something up. So don't worry. I'll do it— for me and for the company."

Sam looked over toward the store. Loomis was still on the porch. He cursed under his breath and turned away, still speaking softly, as if Loomis could hear him from the distance as he answered Jerry's question. "I'm not sure about the woman. My gut feeling is that she doesn't know a damned thing. She doesn't seem the conniving kind." He held the phone away from his ear for Jerry's next tirade.

"I know, looks can be deceiving. We've been fooled before—but not often, and not this time, I guarantee you."

A frown crossed Sam's face. "No, dammit, I'm not falling for her. What the hell gave you that idea?" he asked irritably. "I would never blow something as big as this by getting personally involved. I'm not a rank amateur, after all."

Sam caught himself. "Sorry for losing my temper. It's just the damned heat. And humidity. And wildlife. No, not *night*life—wildlife. They're invading my bedroom, something euphemistically called palmetto bugs that are bigger than Mack trucks. I can't get away from them. All right, I'm exaggerating, but only slightly. And it's not a case of island fever. I'm perfectly sane. I think." Sam laughed ironically.

Then he cupped his hand around the mouthpiece of the phone. "I don't want to sound paranoid, but the old geezer at the store is giving me the once-over so I'm going to hang up. Check out the Santa Luisa thing for me, Jerry. I'll call again as soon as I can."

Sam hung up the phone, wiped his sweaty palms against his shorts and headed for the store. Loomis was rocking and smoking his pipe, eyes bright with interest.

"Hot day to be standing in the sun."

"Had to check in with my office. Even when I'm on vacation, I call now and then. Got a cool drink for me?"

"Sure. Step on in and help you'self out of the cooler. Just leave the money on my counter."

Sam came back on the porch with his bottled soft drink, beaded with drops of water. He downed it in three swallows. "Thanks, Tate."

"Don't mention it. Glad for the business."

"Fireworks were great last night."

Tate took that in stride. "We do right well out here. Heard you was spending the Fourth with Tiger and Gwen and Ali."

Sam smiled. "You heard right. We had a real good time."

"Glad to hear it. They're mighty fine folks."

Sam sighed. Loomis had a one-track mind where the Mallory clan was concerned. "I enjoyed the evening." Sam put his bottle in the wooden carton with the other empties. "Be seeing you, Tate."

He started up the dusty road toward Flattop, wishing that Gwen would come along, pick him up and get him out of the blazing sun.

No, that was not what he was wishing. It was clear to him that he wanted Ali to come along.

"And then what?" he muttered under his breath, no longer surprised when he talked to himself. He was spending so much time alone on Indigo it had become a habit.

He'd lied to his partner, for the first time. Of course he was getting involved with Ali. He was involved since the moment she'd hit him with the hose spray. But even then he'd thought he was just doing a job. Now he knew it was much more complex.

Sam shuffled along in the sandy soil, his sneakers stirring up little clouds of dust. There wasn't a sound except the call of birds and the whir of insect wings. He was very much out of place and very much a stranger here in Ali's world—or the world she had adopted for herself.

5

"SO WHERE WERE YOU all that time?" Gwen asked.

Ali leaned back in her chair. She was sitting opposite Gwen in the Spice of Life office at the big house.

"We took a walk on the beach."

"All that time?"

"Gwen, you don't even know what 'all that time' was. Brian fell asleep immediately. You put him to bed. Then you curled up with a juicy novel."

"Well, maybe I did."

"Tiger was left to clear away the dishes. Afterward, I expect he dozed off in front of the TV."

"Probably," Gwen admitted.

"All that happened in less than an hour."

"Well, an hour's plenty of time to—"

"Gwen." Ali put up her hand. "We walked on the beach and then watched the fireworks. That's it."

"Oh." Gwen was obviously disappointed.

"Well, maybe that's not exactly it."

"Aha." Gwen sat up.

"We talked about the upcoming promotion, and Sam gave me an idea for the Spice of Life ad."

"Ohh," Gwen said.

"Gwen, stop all that aahing and ohing."

"I can't help it. I'm so excited. Let's see the ad."

"Well, it's not just an ad. I'm thinking, if you and Tiger like it, of using this in the brochure and throughout the promotion, to tie everything together. It could be the concept for our whole Christmas marketing campaign." She handed Gwen the mock-up.

Gwen studied it carefully for a long moment and then looked up at Ali. "I love it! This is much more . . . well, more lighthearted and fun than the stuff we've done before. The artwork is adorable with the skating crab. It's very clever, Ali. And to think it was Sam's idea."

"Well, don't get carried away, Gwen. He mentioned shrimp on ice skates and I took it from there."

"But still. How creative, don't you think?"

"Yes, Sam's very creative. Whether he realizes it or not," Ali added.

"And what does he say about all this?"

"I haven't shown it to him."

"Ali!" Gwen sat up straight in her chair. "Why not?"

"May I remind you, Gwen, that I've been working very hard for the past two days on this campaign. Showing it to Sam wasn't high on my priority list. First you and Tiger had to give your okays—"

"We give them as of now."

"Gwen, you can't speak for Tiger."

"Of course I can. Tiger will love it." She handed the mock-ups back to Ali. "Now, let's get back to Sam. Have you been neighborly with him?"

"You know how busy I've been, staying up after midnight for the past two nights. That doesn't give me much time to be neighborly."

"You haven't even seen him?" Gwen was relentless.

"Well, of course I've seen him. He lives next door to me. I see him jogging in the morning before it gets too hot."

"Jogging. Hmm. Now that might be interesting. Nice long legs, broad chest . . ."

"Gwen, you're incorrigible. I'm going to tell Tiger on you."

Gwen laughed, and her eyes sparkled. "Don't bother. Tiger already knows."

Ali joined in the laughter, but she realized Gwen was exactly right about Sam. He did have great legs and a strong, tanned chest and a wonderful rear end. She thought about his hard body and what it had felt like next to hers. She thought about him far too often. All during the day and at night when she lay awake listening to the sea. She imagined Sam in his bed in the cottage nearby.

Ali changed the subject. "Speaking of Tiger, where is my cousin?"

"Speaking of Sam, he's gone crabbing."

"Sam is crabbing with Tiger?"

"And Brian."

"That should be something to see. Can you imagine Sam out there on the tidal river, scooping up crabs with his net?"

"'Course I can. I betcha Sam gets right into it and learns what low-country life is all about. But let's don't speculate. They'll be back shortly so why don't you wait and see?"

"No, thank you, Gwen. I'm going to fax these mock-ups to the mainland, and then I'm heading down to the warehouse to recheck the shipping schedule, and then I'm going to answer the mail, and then—"

"I get the picture," Gwen responded. "No time for Sam Cantrell, but I'm not giving up, because you got along really well at the party, and you went off together. . . ."

"No more speculation, please, Gwen. We got along well because I have good party manners."

"But after the party. . ."

"It doesn't mean anything," Ali insisted, surprised that she could lie so easily to Gwen.

"Of course not," Gwen agreed with mock serious-ness. "You're exactly right, Ali. Having a good time with a great-looking, sexy hunk who happens to live next door to you doesn't mean anything at all."

SAM SAT ON THE FRONT porch of Flattop and sipped a cold beer. At least Loomis could provide that. A faint breeze fought its way off the ocean and almost made it to his porch. Sam was wearing a bathing suit but he wasn't about to go swimming, having discovered that the water was the temperature of a warm bath. And he certainly wasn't going to attempt sailing again. But he'd put on the bathing suit because wearing anything else would be foolish in the heat. Even virtually unclothed, he could feel the perspiration trickling along his ribs.

Sam wondered for the hundredth time why anyone would buy into the fantasy that cottages by the sea were always wafted by ocean breezes. Not this damned cottage. Not Flattop. Vacationers with any sense at all weren't on Indigo Isle; they were in the mountains during the summertime, just as Ali had suggested that first day.

Ali. He had barely caught a glimpse of her since the Fourth of July. She'd made herself very scarce, leaving early in the morning for work and coming home late. After their kiss on the beach, whenever he had managed to approach her, she'd been hurried and even nervous. That wasn't what he had meant to do—scare her off.

"Damn," he muttered under his breath. "This is turning into one hell of a mess." There had been no news from his partner in Atlanta about the possible Santa Luisa connection. And nothing new had turned up on Indigo. He had pumped Tiger and Brian as best he could on their crabbing trek. The result had been two sentences from Tiger.

"Yep, Ali used to be married, but she's a widow now. It's a real sad story, and we just don't like to talk about it." Tiger had quickly turned the conversation to the best way to net crabs, and the moment had been lost.

Sam didn't get the chance again during their afternoon on the river, where he'd spent most of his time trying to avoid the snapping claws of the crabs. Brian and Tiger were adept at catching the squirming little monsters in their nets and dumping them into the bucket of water. Not so Sam. His crabs got caught up in the netting, and when he tried to free them they either clamped down on his hand and held on for dear life or scuttled away along the riverbed, lost forever. After a long day on the river he was still pretty hopeless at crabbing. Equally hopeless at finding out anything about Ali.

Sam took another sip of beer and looked out across the Atlantic Ocean. The moon was rising, full and radiant, and it gave the sand an unearthly sheen. He had to admit it was beautiful, and now that the evening had settled in, there was even a little breeze wafting toward him. He sat back and enjoyed the moment, and when he looked out to sea again, Ali was there.

Sam got up and headed for the beach.

THE TEPID WAVES LAPPED over Ali's feet and gave some relief from the heat. She lifted her heavy hair from her neck and wished for a breeze. Her house had been oppressive. She hadn't been able to work, read or sleep. Even here on the beach her nerves were tightly strung and her skin was feverish.

The rise and fall of the waves, shimmering in the moonlight, intensified her surging restlessness. She gazed up at the moon and wondered if Sam was watching. Would he come to her?

Or would she go to him?

Ali couldn't stop thinking about him and what had begun between them. It couldn't end now. Something had to happen.

She didn't hear him coming; his footsteps were silent in the sand, but she felt his presence before he touched her. Ali swung around to face him, her heart pounding wildly. Her hands were damp with anticipation, and she wiped them on her shorts.

He let his hand remain lightly on her arm. "I've missed you, Ali. Why are you hiding from me?"

"Hiding?" Her voice had a catch in it, maybe because of what he said but more likely because of how he looked. She saw his face clearly in the moonlight and felt the same magic she'd noticed before. Moonlight did that to the strongly etched planes of Sam's cheekbones, the dark wings of his eyebrows. It played havoc with the glitter of his sea green eyes. She took a step away and then stopped. They'd played this game before. Now it was time to be honest.

"Yes, I've been hiding because…" She swallowed hard and went on in a nearly desperate voice, her words torn from her. "Don't you know why?"

Sam's response was to take her in his arms and pull her close. His mouth was hot and seeking. Ali opened her lips under his, letting his kiss flow through her. She was hungry for him, for the remembered pleasure of his touch, the passion of his kisses and the feeling of his body against hers.

"You have witchcraft in your kisses, Ali," he murmured against her hair. "And magic in your body." Sam ran his hands up and down her back, under her blouse. The blood pounded in his head, and any rational thought he might have had was pushed away by the hot rush of passion. They'd kissed like this before, but something was different tonight. "Witchcraft," he repeated.

"No," she murmured under his kisses. "You're the sorcerer."

"If I'm the sorcerer—" he kissed her words away "—then let me execute my powers."

"Sam—"

"Yes. Listen to the sorcerer. I want to make love to you, Ali. I want to take you to my bed and hold you, kiss you, love you." His voice was rough with passion.

Ali's arms were tight around his neck, her mouth close to his. "This is crazy," she murmured.

She was right, Sam thought. It was crazy, wild and absolutely wonderful. He wanted Ali more than anything, and he wasn't going to let her go. Damn the job, to hell with the consequences.

"All I do is think about you, Ali. Every minute since I met you. Every second since I kissed you."

"I think about you, too, Sam." Her voice was so soft he had to strain to hear the words. "All the time."

Relief flooded through him. He kissed her forehead and cheek, her eyelids and then her ear, exploring the sensitive skin with his tongue. Ali squirmed in his arms, moaning softly, her body pressed against his.

She drew his mouth to hers and drank deeply of his kisses. Her tongue pushed against the inner recesses of his mouth. Her lips were hot on his, and she clung to him, burying her hands in his hair, holding him close.

Without a word Sam picked her up and walked across the beach. She seemed light as a feather in his arms. He moved over the sand quickly, his heart pounding, his knees weak, and made it through the sea oats that grew in the dunes around his cottage. Finally he reached the steps leading to his porch.

As Sam struggled to open the door, Ali slid out of his arms, along the length of his body. She stood molded against him, her arms around his waist, her mouth raised to his.

They kissed, swaying against each other in a kind of sensuous dance. The kiss was long and slow, a thorough exploration, and when it ended Ali's lips were bruised and tingly, damp with Sam's moisture.

Then they were kissing again, and this time she gave herself even more completely to him, nibbling, licking, sucking on his lips.

Sam knew he would never make it into the house, certainly not as far as his bed. "Ali..." he began. He saw her face in the moonlight. Desire was etched in her eyes. Her mouth was soft and vulnerable, her lips parted, the red tip of her tongue protruding slightly.

He watched her in fascination as she sank to the steps and held out her arms to him.

He knelt on the step below her. "You're so beautiful in the moonlight." He touched her face with wonder, moved his fingertips down the line of her neck, her bare arms. Then he tugged at the soft fabric of her shirt. She helped him pull it over her head and toss it carelessly into the sand.

Ali felt the warm breeze across her skin and then Sam's hand against her nipple, just the gentlest brush of his palm, and yet it caused an unexpected friction. She caught her breath as desire rippled along her spine. Then his mouth was on her other breast, hot and moist and sensual.

Ali couldn't stop the little whimpers of pleasure that rose from deep within. With his mouth Sam traced a path between her breasts, and with his hands he pulled at her shorts until the buttons gave way.

She felt the rough cotton denim rubbing against her legs as he slid off the shorts. For a moment they tangled at her ankles, but Ali kicked them away into the sand beside her T-shirt.

She fumbled in the dark, caught the string of Sam's bathing suit in her hand and gave it a quick yank. He pulled the suit down, and Ali touched his swollen manhood. It was hot and hard. She ran her hand along the length of him, caressed him, held him. She felt him grow beneath her fingers.

She was consumed by the sensations that pulsed through her, turning her hotter than the hottest summer night, controlling her totally.

"Tell me what you want, Ali."

He leaned toward her, bracing his hands on each side of her naked body. She was open to him, exposed. But Ali couldn't answer his question; she could hardly breathe. There were only her feelings and Sam and the hot summer breeze against her skin.

She guided him toward her, and an instant after she felt the tip of his manhood rub against her she opened to welcome him. He entered her, and their eyes met and locked.

Sam's eyes were dark with desire, and his look stirred something in Ali that had been lying lost and dormant.

She felt a deep primitive blossoming, an awakening that flowed and merged with the heat of Sam's body.

He thrust inside her. He meant to be more gentle, but his need consumed him and pushed away all thoughts. When she moved toward him, shifted and encompassed him totally, Sam's body caught fire from hers. He thrust again and again, and each time her body matched his in rhythm and intensity.

Ali felt the relentless surge of her pleasure, like a wave rushing for the shore, drawing her backward in the riptide, and then moving on furiously, frantically.

Her fingers dug into his shoulders, and her sounds of ecstasy multiplied and grew as his body exploded inside her, leaving joy and fulfillment in its wake.

THE SOUND OF RIPPLING waves broke the spell as night slowly came into focus. The black velvet sky above filled with stars. The silver path of the moon raced across the water. The frogs and crickets in the brush and woods came to life.

Ali hid her face against Sam's neck and tried to catch her breath. She felt the heat emanating from his body, his wet skin against her, his rough whiskers rubbing her face. Their hot, sticky bodies were still joined. She was naked on the steps, and he was on top of her.

"Are you all right?" he asked huskily.

"Yes, I'm wonderful."

He laughed. "You are that. But the steps. You probably have splinters up and down your body." He rolled over and pulled her on top of him. "Now I get the splinters."

"Do you feel them?" she asked.

"No." He hugged her close.

"Neither did I."

"I meant to take you to my bed."

"It was perfect this way."

Sam smiled against her warm, damp body. "Perfect," he repeated. "Even on the steps."

"I only felt you."

"Oh, Ali." Sam held her tightly on top of him, and Ali relaxed on his body. She was happy there. She didn't want to be separated. There was something safe and secure about lying so comfortably on him. There was something wonderful about having his arms securely around her, belonging to her, if only for a while.

He shifted, enveloping her completely, his legs around hers. He kissed her hair. "The night isn't over, Ali. I want to love you again, slowly this time. I want to taste your delicious long legs. I want to lick your wonderful thighs."

"You make me sound like a meal," she teased.

"Maybe sex is the spice of life. Have you thought about that?"

They looked at each other and laughed. "Not until this minute," she said. Their laughter grew, and in the midst of it Sam sat up, still holding her securely. He settled on the stair and shifted her easily into his lap.

"What would the neighbors say about you sitting here naked on my front steps?"

"What neighbors?"

"I guess we're our own neighbors," Sam said as he nibbled her neck.

"I won't tell if you don't."

"Never," he agreed. "Not even when we take a shower to cool off and then get all heated up again." Sam cupped her breast in his hand. He loved the soft, heavy feel of it against him.

"I have a better idea. Let's skinny-dip to cool off, and then get heated up."

"You're full of surprises, Ali. What Gwen and Tiger told me was true."

"Don't believe anything they say," she teased. Then she asked curiously, "What *did* they say?"

"That you were an impetuous firebrand. And that's a direct quote."

"I'd hate to make liars out of them." Her lips found his, and her tongue glided along his teeth. "Let's go for a swim and then get all hot and bothered again." Her body, damp with passion, molded against his.

Sam felt desire returning, curling and twisting inside him. He ran his hand along her silky thigh. "Why, Ali, I think you're a hedonist," he said in mock dismay. "A nice Southern lady like you?"

"Sam, honey, don't you know all this heat gets me stirred up?" she asked in her most sugary Southern voice.

"Well, all I can say is that it took you long enough to get hot and bothered."

"And it'll take just as long to cool down." She kissed the tip of his nose. "I'd say we have a long hot night ahead of us."

THE SHEETS WERE COOL against her skin. Overhead, the blades of a ceiling fan wafted streams of tepid air around the bed. A dim light filtered in from the living room. As Sam came through the door, Ali reached for the sheet to cover herself.

"Cold?" Sam must have known she couldn't possibly be cold, but she also couldn't be as perfectly at ease as he was, standing there totally nude before her. He walked around the bed just as easily, sat beside her and placed a pitcher of ice water and two glasses on the bedside table.

Ali shook her head. "Nope. Just kind of . . ."

"Shy?" Sam slipped into bed beside her. "No, you couldn't possibly be shy after what happened to us on the steps." He ran his hand carelessly along her hip.

Ali snuggled close to him. "Maybe not shy but just a little unsure." Her voice trembled slightly. "You're the first man I've made love to since . . . since my husband."

He put his arm around her. "I'm so glad that I was here. I'm glad it was with me."

"So am I." She sighed in contentment, letting her fingers drift along the muscles of his shoulder and chest. She touched his scar and let her hand rest there. "Are you going to tell me about this?"

"Do you really want me to?"

"Of course. You know all about me. It's only fair that I learn something about Sam Cantrell."

"Yes, I suppose you're right. Mine isn't a very pretty story."

"If you remember, neither was mine."

He stretched out beside her and held her close. "I remember," he said. "About the scar . . ." He paused a moment and then said quickly without hesitation, "Okay, it's from a gunshot wound."

Ali swallowed hard. "I thought so. I mean, it looked so . . . sinister."

"In case you're wondering, and I know you are, I wasn't the bad guy, Ali. I was a cop, a young cop who got involved in a shoot-out. I was lucky to get through it alive."

There was something in his voice that warned Ali not to ask more questions. But she couldn't help making an observation. "A policeman. You were a policeman?"

"Just briefly," he answered. "After the army. Then I got wounded and decided I needed to look for a healthier way of life."

"I guess insurance is pretty healthy," she commented, curious about the transformation in careers but again not questioning him directly.

"Healthy, yes, except when we overwork."

"So you've come here to recover."

"From exertion, not a gunshot wound this time. My work can be grueling, even boring sometimes."

"And—"

He kissed her on the nose without further comment.

"So you're not going to tell me all about yourself."

"Not now. Not when I have a long-legged, sexy woman in bed with me."

"Sam—" Her curiosity couldn't be denied.

"Tomorrow, I promise. You'll know everything about Sam Cantrell tomorrow. But right now all I can think about is this long-legged woman, whom I promised to do something to. Now, what was it?"

In the light that filtered in from the living room Ali could see the flickering of desire in Sam's eyes, and it was answered by her own heightened awareness. Her skin tingled with remembered passion.

"Now I know what it was, something about tasting you all over." He kissed her lips and then slowly, deliberately, kissed the hollow between her breasts before taking one nipple in his mouth. "Just as I expected," he said. "Pink and delicate and perfect."

While his hand caressed her, he let his lips drift downward to the round softness of her tummy, the line of her hipbone, the curve of her knee. "Mustn't forget your toes." He kissed each one lovingly, and then her instep, her ankle, the curve of her calf.

His warm breath continued to caress her gently, his tongue to taste the salty skin of her body. Ali closed her eyes and let him work his magic on her.

She squirmed under his touch, urging him on with whispered murmurs of delight and pleasure. He teased the inside of her thigh with his tongue and finally reached the center of her desire. There he used his lips and tongue to take her to the edge of ecstasy and bring her back again. It was torture, divine torment, this slow, erotic exploration.

Ali cupped his head in her hands, holding him, running her fingers through his dark hair. Her body was hot and flooded with need down to her fingertips.

He looked up and saw the passion on her face, felt the heat emanating from her body, merging into him. Her fingers dug into the muscles of his shoulders and pulled him upward along her body as she leaned forward to meet him. Her breath, short and ragged, found its rhythm in his. Sam willed himself to move slowly in spite of his need.

"Ali. My beautiful Ali. I want to be with you, to love you...."

She pulled him closer, kissed his face and then his lips, long and hard. Then she shifted beneath him so he could slide into her and fill her with his manhood. At that movement of supreme contact, she caressed his buttocks, dug her fingernails into his spine, wrapped her legs around his back and drew him even closer.

Sam smiled at the sight of her face, filled with pleasure and a kind of sensual innocence that made his heart twist inside him. He would tell her everything tomorrow, but now he could think only of making love to her, touching her, giving her pleasure. This was his fantasy; he was living it now as he became locked together with Ali in the wondrous dance of love.

They moved slowly, almost dreamily. "I'm going to love you all night long, Ali," he murmured, his breath warm against her cheek.

"Oh," she cried, "I hope that's a promise you'll keep."

She raised her hips to meet his slow, undulating thrusts, closed her eyes and let the magic of their love-making engulf her.

ALI STEPPED OUT of the shower and reached for a towel. She dried herself slowly, thoughtfully, reliving the long night with Sam. She'd awakened alone in bed, momen-tarily confused about where she was. Then she'd re-membered, had heard the sounds of Sam whistling in the kitchen as he clattered pots and pans, had smiled to her-self and determined to join him, but not until she had her shower.

Wrapped in the towel, she caught a glimpse of herself in the mirror. Her lips were bruised from his kisses, and there was a red mark on her neck. She laughed aloud. No doubt about it, she looked just like what she was—a woman who'd been loved all night long. She felt like purring with satisfaction. Sam had been the most won-derful of lovers—gentle, passionate, giving. Even in the bright light of day she had no regrets about becoming his lover. Not one.

She padded to the closet and looked for something to slip on. Sam wouldn't be the kind of man to own a bath-robe, she decided, but one of his shirts would do. She reached for a white shirt on the nearest hanger, pulled it out and started to slip it on.

That's when she saw the gun. It was hanging in a hol-ster at the back of the closet.

She froze, a frisson of fear racing along her spine. Why a gun? What did he need it for on Indigo Isle? She quickly backed away and closed the closet door. He had been a policeman, after all, she told herself. Maybe ex-policemen kept their guns. Or maybe he hadn't been a policeman at all. Maybe . . .

She didn't know what to think but, determined to find out, she slipped on his shirt and pushed open the door to the front room that overlooked the Atlantic. Sunlight bounced off the shimmering waves, and she blinked for a moment in the glare. Then she saw Sam at the kitchen door, chest bare, wearing khaki shorts, stirring a bowl of eggs.

"Well, good morning, sleepyhead. The coffee is on, and your omelet will be ready soon. I cook a great breakfast." He looked at her more closely. "Okay, that's not quite correct, but my omelet is eatable." After another pause he seemed to catch on. "Is something the matter?"

"I don't know." Ali took a step toward the kitchen. "I borrowed a shirt."

"You look great in it."

"There was a gun in your closet," she blurted out quickly.

Sam nodded.

"I didn't mean to pry."

"I'm sure you didn't," Sam agreed.

"I was looking for something to wear." She noticed her own clothes neatly folded on a chair. "Why a gun, Sam? You're not a policeman anymore."

She finally looked directly at him, and the expression on his face made her heart stop in midbeat. It was a look of sadness and guilt and maybe even fear. "Sam, what is it?"

He came into the front room, still holding the bowl, and moved toward her, his eyes on hers. "I meant to tell you sooner. I should have—before we made love—but I couldn't. Not then. I made up my mind to tell you everything today. Remember? I said I would."

"I remember," she mouthed.

"I didn't mean for this to get so confused."

Ali backed away from him, just as she'd backed out of the closet when she saw the gun. She reached out and grabbed a chair to steady herself. "Tell me now, Sam."

"I was a policeman. And I'm not anymore. That part's true."

"And the rest is a lie?"

"No. Not the way I feel about you, but . . ."

Ali felt as if a cold hand had compressed her heart.

"I'm a private investigator."

She felt the blood drain from her face.

"Your husband's company hired me to find the money."

Ali raised a hand to her mouth as if to stem a scream. "And now you're investigating me! You came here to trap me, and you made love to me."

Sam was across the room in two strides. He grasped her shoulders and gave her a little shake. "It wasn't that way, Ali. We need to talk. You need to listen to me—"

She twisted out of his grip, hurled herself across the room and out the door. Sam hesitated half a second and then ran after her.

Ali's long legs ate up the distance in the soft, clinging sand. She was running along the beach toward her house as Sam charged behind her.

"Ali, Ali! Stop. Listen. We need to talk!"

She kept on running. Sam gave up shouting at her and lengthened his stride. She was an arm's length away now. A hand. A fingertip. He grabbed for the flapping hem of the shirt and pulled her to the sand. She dropped sprawling, and Sam fell on top of her.

6

Sam pinned Ali in the sand, holding her arms above her head. She bucked furiously beneath him, but he braced himself and dug his feet into the sand. "You're going to listen to me, Ali. Dammit, you're going to listen."

"You had all week to tell me who you are. It's too late now!" Her eyes flashed fire at him.

"I didn't want to tell you until I got to know you."

She looked as though she wanted to spit in his face. "Well, you got to know me, all right, Mr. Detective. I imagine you had a few secret little laughs last night about just how easy I was to know." She kicked out wildly, but Sam held on, determined to make her listen.

"I didn't have any laughs at all because there was nothing funny about last night. It was all true and real, but I couldn't tell you then. That would have spoiled our time together. I planned to tell you everything this morning."

"Yeah, sure. If I hadn't found that gun of yours—"

"The gun had nothing to do with it, Ali. I told you last night, long before you found the gun, that you'd know everything about me today. I meant it then, and I mean it now."

She lay quiet, tired of struggling, but Sam stayed on top of her, afraid that she'd make a break and he'd lose his chance.

"I was hired by Westfield Investments because they want to get back the money that Casey stole. It's that simple."

"I don't have it," she said through gritted teeth.

"Westfield doesn't know that. You were Casey's wife. This seemed the logical place to start. Obviously, if I'd announced who I was, you would hardly have welcomed me onto Indigo Isle."

"So you decided to lie your way on like the weasel you are."

"That was part of my M.O. I didn't consider it lying."

"But it *was* lying." She glared at him. "Now let me up. Your hipbone is digging into my side."

Sam shifted slightly but kept his weight against her. "We're staying here until I finish. I came to Indigo as part of a job. I'm sure you can understand that. You're ambitious, you work hard. This was a big account, a big client. It could move our firm from the midlist to the top. So I took the damn job. I didn't know you. I didn't know anything about you. What was I supposed to do, Ali— blurt everything out to a woman I'd never seen in my life?"

Ali ignored the question. "You used me. You used my family. You abused their hospitality. You're disgusting and lower than a snake's belly, Sam Cantrell, if that's even your name."

"It is my name, and I was doing my job."

"You don't eat at the table of your enemy."

"You're not my enemy, Ali, and neither are Gwen and Tiger. I like them very much. Brian, too. He's a great kid."

Sam let his guard down for a moment, and Ali rolled over and sat up. She was covered with sand. It was down her back, in her hair, even in her mouth. She wiped her lips with the back of her hand and Sam's big shirt gaped open, displaying the curve of her breast. Intent on getting up and getting out of there, she didn't even bother to button the shirt.

But Sam had shifted, too, and now his legs were over hers. She tried kicking them off to no avail. He held on firmly to one of her arms at the wrist. "When Tiger and Gwen hear the facts, they'll understand. So will you."

"I've heard the facts, Sam."

"Not all of them."

"Enough," she cried. "And they'll understand just what I do, that you're a rat of the first order."

"Then let me tell you the rest of the facts, Ms. Ali Paxton Bell." He grabbed her other wrist and looked her directly in the eye, his face only inches away. "As long as the money is missing, you're going to be a suspect. You were his wife, for God's sake. The only way you'll ever get free of Casey Bell and his ghost is to prove your innocence. If we find the money, you can do that. Or had you rather stay shackled to a dead man for the rest of your life?" He took her by the shoulders and gave her a little shake. "Is that what you want—to keep running and hiding and never face up to reality, never know the truth?"

"I know the truth. The truth is that I'm innocent. I don't need a two-bit ex-policeman to prove it." Her voice dripped with venom.

Stung by her words, Sam dropped his hands. She wiggled out from under his legs and got away, retreating backward in the sand like a crab. "I don't know anything about Casey's money," she said as she moved.

Sam followed her on his hands and knees but didn't grab her again. They were both covered with sand, crouched in it like two wild animals eyeing each other for battle.

"I don't know where the money is. I've said that from the beginning. I can't make it any clearer, and no matter how many times you make love to me, you won't make me change my story."

His anger caught fire from hers. "Dammit, Ali, that's not why I made love to you!" Sam sat back on his heels. "Meeting you, getting to know you, making love— Oh, Ali, that was something separate and special. It had nothing to do with Casey and the money."

Ali struggled to her feet and looked down at him. Sam was reminded of a queen surveying one of her less fortunate subjects. "The money has everything to do with it, Sam. It's all about money and betrayal. It has damn little to do with making love."

She turned on her heel and stalked toward her cottage, and as Sam watched her go he sank back into the sand, feeling as bad as he'd ever felt in his life.

"WHY, SAM CANTRELL'S nothing but a skunk!" Gwen's voice quivered with righteous indignation, and her freckled face reddened with anger. "I can't believe he'd lie to us like that!"

Gwen rocked in her old green rocking chair on the big house porch. Tiger was in the swing, a serious look on his face, and Ali sat on the steps, leaning against the porch column. "Well, lie he did," she responded.

"If you want him off this island, he'll be gone by noon. Tiger wasn't a lawyer for twenty years without learning how to get rid of an unwanted renter, were you, Tiger?"

Her husband nodded.

Gwen looked at Ali with apology in her eyes. "To think that I encouraged a romance—that is, a friendship—between the two of you. Thank the good Lord you had more sense than to listen to—" Gwen broke off, seeing the look on Ali's face.

Ali realized that her cousin knew by the inadvertent expression that something had happened. To hide her flush of embarrassment, she stood and crossed the porch. "He's a pro, Gwen. He fooled all of us." She pushed open the screen door and went inside, heading for the kitchen. She could hear Gwen and Tiger talking in low, animated voices.

Ali put a low flame under the coffeepot. Sun streamed through the windows of the big, old-fashioned kitchen. From the backyard came the sounds of Brian and his friends playing, the barking of dogs. The kitchen was filled with the scent of Tiger's special blend of coffee. It was just a normal, average summer day. Except her life was turned upside down again.

Tiger and Gwen had come into the kitchen and settled quietly at the table.

"Coffee?" Ali asked. She was composed now as she turned to face them. They both nodded.

Ali touched the pot to make sure it was warm, got down three cups from the cabinet and poured the coffee. Tiger took two cups back to the table.

"Now that we know what he's up to, the question is, what do you want to do about him?" Tiger asked.

Ali remained standing at the counter. "Do about him? For starters, how about cutting him up in little pieces and using him for shark bait?" She stalked over to the table and sat down.

Gwen touched her arm. "I'm pleased to hear you talking that way, Ali."

"If you like it, there's more where that came from. Let's use his toes for crab bait, while he's still attached to them. Let's—"

Gwen smiled at the image. "What I meant is that I'm glad to see you all angry and stirred up. Why, last time you were so depressed over Casey, we thought you'd never get your gumption back."

Ali made a scornful, hissing sound through her teeth. "Thanks a lot for reminding me that I have a talent for getting myself hooked up with rats. That's certainly very comforting."

"Oh, goodness, I didn't mean that, either," Gwen protested. "I meant that it's much healthier to be angry than depressed. You've come a long way, and together we'll think of some way to get even with Mr. Sam Cantrell. Isn't that what the politicians say, Tiger—don't get mad, get even?"

"That's what they say."

"Well, I'm already good and mad. Now I'd like to get even, too," Ali told them.

Tiger sipped his coffee thoughtfully, and Ali looked over at him. "You've been awfully noncommittal, Tiger."

He put down the mug and spoke slowly and deliberately. "I reckon it would be a good idea to think about this. Let's analyze the situation before we feed Sam to the sharks."

"Don't tell me you're sympathetic to the awful man," Gwen said.

"Don't jump to conclusions, Gwen. I'm a lawyer. I like to look at every angle."

"That's the Lord's truth," Gwen said.

"Then listen to me. Sam was hired to find Casey's money. In the long run that could be beneficial to Ali. If he's successful, her name could be cleared once and for all."

"He's not going to find it here," Ali stated adamantly.

"We know Ali is perfectly innocent," Gwen put in.

Tiger put up a conciliatory hand. "We know that, but Sam doesn't. Or didn't. He had to start somewhere, and this was the logical place."

Ali cringed at the explanation, identical to Sam's.

"Besides, I expect Sam realizes she's innocent now. Else, why this confession to her?"

Ali didn't like the lawyer's mind working things out, but she kept her mouth shut, determined not to say a word about her night in bed with Sam.

"Maybe he thought he'd been found out?" Gwen suggested.

"Could be," Tiger mused. "You know, Ali, honey, you might think about looking at this Sam fellow as an opportunity instead of a problem."

"Not a chance," Ali said flatly.

"Hear me out. He's obviously a top-flight investigator. I can vouch for that. Otherwise, Westfield wouldn't have hired him. It's a very professional firm. Now, his investigation on the mainland led to you."

"I'm a dead end, Tiger, and you know it."

"Maybe . . . just maybe . . . Sam could jog your memory or uncover some fact you haven't been able to remember up to now."

"Tiger, you're not saying Ali should work with the man?"

"Hear me out, Gwen. I'm simply quoting Grandmother, who used to tell Ali and me, 'Don't bite off your nose to spite your face.' So let's don't throw Sam off the island just yet. He might be of some help to us."

"Humph," Ali snorted.

"He used you. Now use him. Get to the bottom of this Casey thing once and for all."

"I see what you mean," Gwen said. "He might be able to help Ali."

"Not you, too, Gwen!"

"Now, Ali," Gwen soothed, "Tiger could be right. It's possible that Sam is a blessing in disguise."

"That blessing in disguise is more like wolf in sheep's clothing," Ali snapped.

"Just think about it for a while. Then if you still want him off the island, let me know, and Sam Cantrell will be history," Tiger promised.

Ali chewed thoughtfully on her bottom lip. Despite all the hurt and anger she was feeling, Sam's words kept ringing in her head. "He said the only way I'd be free of Casey's ghost was to prove I was innocent, and finding the money would do that."

"He's right," Tiger said.

"I feel like I'd be jumping out of the frying pan and into the fire."

Gwen laughed. "I guess it's my turn to offer up a little homily. How about 'nothing ventured, nothing gained'? If Sam Cantrell, lying snake that he is, gives you the opportunity to end this Casey nightmare once and for all, then reach out for it, honey. Life's too short to sit on the sidelines and watch it all go by."

WHEN ALI GOT OUT of the car she saw him sitting on her back steps. Without a break in her stride she crossed the yard, her expression resolute and unreadable.

Sam stood and reached out to touch her arm. She shrugged past him up the stairs.

"I see you had the sense to wear sandals to protect you from the sandspurs," she observed.

"Ali, I need to talk to you."

She opened the door and gestured him in. "And I want to talk to you, Cantrell."

Taken aback by her easy acquiescence, Sam followed her into the kitchen. Ali opened the refrigerator and took out a bottle of white wine. She poured a glass and then looked at him. "Wine?"

"Sure. Yes." Maybe that would help. Maybe the wine would take the edge off her anger and make her a little more understanding.

"Let's go into the living room." It was more of an order than an invitation.

He followed, wondering what the hell was going on. He'd expected her to be cold, hostile, angry. She wasn't exactly friendly, but at least she was talking. That was a good sign. He was grateful for anything at this point. Sam sat down to wait. It was her show now.

Ali sat across from him, her face serious, eyes shadowed. "I've talked with Tiger and Gwen about you."

Inwardly he groaned, but Sam kept his face impassive. "Is the lynch mob on its way?"

"If I request it."

He shivered dramatically at the ice in her voice, but Ali didn't crack a smile.

"Tiger, who was—and still is—one of the best lawyers in the state, has offered me some advice."

Sam drank his wine and waited. This could go either way.

"He suggested that despite your deceit, trickery, lying and all-around snakelike behavior, you might actually be of some help to me."

"You mean in finding the money?"

"Exactly."

"I told you that last night."

"Yes, and some of what you said on the beach makes sense in the light of day."

"And with Tiger's corroboration?"

Ali nodded and sipped her wine in silence for a moment. "As long as the money is missing, guilt and doubt are going to be attached to my name. Maybe there is some way I can help you. Maybe since time has passed, I'll have a better perspective on things. Something might come to mind. Anyway, I've decided to cooperate, even help if I can. I want Casey's ghost out of my life."

Sam gave a big sigh of relief. All wasn't lost. Not with the case and maybe not even with Ali.

She went on. "If we find the money, then I want it made clear that I'm innocent."

There was something in the way she phrased her demand that caused him to hesitate momentarily.

She jumped into the silence. "Or maybe you don't think I'm innocent?"

"All I want is to find out what really happened. That's my job. It's why I came here."

"Then we're agreed," she said.

"There's more to it, Ali, more we need to talk about. There's last night and . . . us."

She shook her head emphatically. "You couldn't be more wrong, detective. There isn't any *us*. No Sam and Ali. And as for last night, let's forget it ever happened." Her voice almost wavered, but she recovered quickly. "I was as much at fault as you. Blame it on the moonlight."

"Fault, blame? That's not how I remember last night," he said stubbornly.

"Then our recollections differ."

"I don't like the way that sounds, Ali."

"Sam, I'm not going to talk about it, or think about what a fool I was."

"Ali, please . . ." He reached out and put his hand on her knee.

She pulled back and held up a warning hand. "If you want us to work together, then it has to be strictly business."

Sam got up and stood next to her chair, looking down at her. His body was too close for comfort, but Ali didn't move, didn't let him know she was uneasy.

"There's still going to be something between us, Ali. It's there."

"Maybe for you," she said. "Not for me." She didn't look at him. "Last night happened, there's no denying that, but it's over now and best forgotten."

"I'm not going to forget."

She looked up then and smiled a cool little smile. "Why, Sam, aren't you the one who talks about moving on and laying the past to rest?"

Sam gritted his teeth. She had him playing by her rules, and he hated that. He moved away and sat back down in his chair.

"You're here to solve a case, Sam. You've said that yourself."

She still had him. He didn't respond.

"I'm very clear where I stand, but if you're not, maybe you need to go back to Atlanta."

"I'm a professional, Ali, and if you want a business deal, that's what you'll get."

She studied him suspiciously for a moment and then shrugged. "All I have is your word, which I know can't be trusted." It wasn't going to be easy trusting her own feelings, either, but Ali was determined to succeed. "But your word will have to do for now," she said. "Where do we start?"

He thought of the box he'd seen in the spare bedroom. "Do you have any of Casey's belongings—letters, diaries, notes, telephone logs? Anything like that would give us a hint of what he had on his mind."

"The police and the feds went through all that stuff at the house."

"But you brought it with you?"

"Yes, for some perverse reason. Maybe I even thought I'd go through it all again someday, when I had distanced myself from the whole mess. I guess I had the idea that there really might be some clue."

"If there is, we'll find it together." His voice was assured and somehow made Ali feel better, but her emotions were still frayed. So much was happening at once, including her feelings for Sam, which had gone from early annoyance to deep desire and finally to outright anger. She'd have to keep all those emotions in check. Then there was the past to deal with again, being let down by Casey, and now having to go back through the very things that reminded her of him.

"It may not be easy," Sam said.

He must have seen the confusion in her eyes. Ali blinked it away. She could get through this. She had to. "There's a box in the bedroom," she announced. "I guess we can start there."

ALI SAT in a canvas-backed chair sipping her wine while Sam began pulling items out of the box—scrapbooks, photos, memorabilia from Casey's college days, notes of sympathy to Ali from friends and family after Casey's death. "I know this is painful for you," he said.

"I can handle it." How she felt about Casey and the past was not Sam's business right now, she decided.

Sam glanced through the photographs. The Bell house in Atlanta, two-story brick on a lawn so green it seemed painted. Azaleas blooming along the curved driveway. The white shine of dogwoods in blossom. The pictures portrayed a life of elegance and ease. He sifted through photos of Casey and Ali beside their pool, in the garden, drinking champagne at a party. He was tall, blond, well dressed and very good-looking. In one of the pictures he held Ali proprietarily close.

"Golden boy," Sam murmured softly.

"I imagine you came across that phrase in your research. It's what the newspapers called him. Everything came so easily to Casey, or so it seemed. In fact, nothing was paid for. We were in debt for all of it—a beautiful glossy veneer."

"But he was successful. Eventually he would have—"

"Oh, yes. Eventually. But Casey couldn't wait. He wanted it all and he wanted it immediately."

"How did you meet him, or do you want to talk about that?"

"I don't mind," Ali said. "We met at a party during our junior year in college." Ali talked about their college days while Sam continued going through the box.

"Was he flamboyant even then?"

"Oh, yes, and very charismatic. Charisma." She said it slowly. "I'd heard that word before but never known what it meant until I met him. It was an aura that surrounded him and made him seem like the man to emulate. He was in the best fraternity, all the clubs that mattered, and of course he was president of the student body in our senior year."

"How about his grades, was he a good student?"

Ali smiled. "Casey never had much time for studying, but he managed to sail through quite easily. I wouldn't be surprised if he had friends writing his papers for him in those classes that didn't matter, that wouldn't help further his career."

Ali walked over to the window and looked out at the ocean. "He had our life all planned out—move to Atlanta, get great jobs, have a wonderful house and lots of friends, eventually raise a family. . . ."

Sam was almost at the bottom of the box. In two hours of going over the contents, with Ali filling in the details, he'd learned something about Casey Bell's life. But he hadn't found anything to shed light on what had happened to the half million dollars.

"What's this?" He pulled out a book. "It's a Bible." Casey's name was stamped in gold on the front. "I'd never have imagined him to be religious."

"The Bible is from his childhood. And you're right, he wasn't much of a churchgoer, but he liked the architecture, the ceremony, the pomp and circumstance, I suppose. Casey adored splendor, and whenever we traveled he always visited cathedrals and churches."

Ali took the Bible from Sam. "I don't know why I kept this except that there was no one else to take it. No relatives other than his mother, who's in a retirement home in Arizona and doesn't want to be reminded of him."

"What happened to everything else?"

"I suppose you mean the valuable things—the house, cars, furnishings? I sold it all to pay off debts. This box is what I have left of Casey."

Sam took the Bible and paged through it. A letter fell out, and he picked it up. "May I read this?"

"You're the detective, so I imagine you will, anyway."

Sam unfolded the flimsy pages and looked at the date. "December thirtieth. Ali, he wrote this six days after he disappeared—while he was still in hiding on Santa Luisa." Sam felt his heart quicken with excitement.

"I didn't get it immediately, though. It was here, waiting for me when I came to Indigo. He mailed it directly to Spice of Life."

"So the letter never went to Atlanta?"

Ali's lips turned down in a smirk. "For a detective, you have a way of repeating the obvious. No, the letter never went to Atlanta. I was there. It came here. I read it weeks later, after the funeral."

Sam couldn't contain the skepticism in his voice. "How did Casey know you'd come to Indigo?"

"Because he knew me. He knew that after what he'd done there'd be publicity, a furor, and I'd run for sanctuary. It wasn't part of a master plan, if that's what you're thinking. In fact, I'd forgotten all about the letter."

Sam turned it over in his hands carefully but still didn't read it. First he looked through the other things left in the box. "No envelope," he said.

"Another grasp of the obvious. I gave the stamps to Brian and then I suppose I threw the envelope away. There wasn't a return address, just my name printed in block letters. Gwen didn't even pay any attention to it when it arrived, just put it in with all the sympathy cards and letters of condolence that she saved for me in a box at the big house."

"Did you throw the envelope away before or after you showed the letter to the police?"

Her answer came slowly. "I never showed it to the police."

"You never—" He stopped in midsentence and willed himself to keep his voice calm. "Why not, Ali?"

"Because Casey was dead and buried, because it was personal, because it couldn't have been of any interest to them. And mostly because I couldn't take any more."

She went back to her chair and sat down. "Can't you understand that, Sam? I was at the end of my rope then. I simply couldn't stand one more encounter with the police."

Sam looked down at the letter and then back up at Ali.

"Go ahead, read it. You'll see that it says nothing about what he did with the money at all. If he had given the slightest hint, I would have called the police. But he didn't—and I didn't. And dammit, by then I deserved some peace. Go ahead," she ordered, "read it and see for yourself."

Sam's suspicions were running rampant as he skimmed the letter.

It was long and convoluted. In the first part Casey poured out his love for Ali. Sam read snatches of it aloud.

"I know it will work out for us . . . we can be together . . . I'm counting on it. . . . I didn't mean for it to happen this way, but we can make a new life. Without you, I couldn't go on, but we'll still have everything we dreamed of. . . ."

Sam looked up at Ali in surprise. "He thought you were going to join him?"

Ali shook her head sadly. "I've realized that my husband was not only an egotist—I guess I knew that all along—but a sociopath, as well. He really didn't think there was anything particularly wrong with what he did and imagined I'd feel the same—that it was all justified.

He assumed I'd join him and we'd run off to God knows where, take new names and live happily ever after."

"You didn't know anything about his plans, not even the assumed name he used in Santa Luisa?"

Anger flashed in Ali's eyes. "I told you I knew nothing!" She paused. "And how did you know about the fake name, anyway?"

"It was in all the papers, Ali—Allen Riley. Does it mean anything to you?"

"No, it doesn't, as I told the police, which was also in all the papers. I'm tired of the questions, Sam." Ali slumped back in her chair.

"I'm afraid they're necessary for me to interpret this." He waved the letter. "It's pretty strange, a kind of love letter and travelogue—what he did, what he saw, where he stayed and ate, all mixed with long paragraphs about his love for you."

"It was the only letter he ever wrote me. I had nothing to compare it to, but yes, it was strange, almost as if he planned to return to Santa Luisa someday and begin his life over with me beside him."

"Exactly," Sam said. "But you'd never talked with him about that possibility?"

"Dammit, Sam, I'm tired of the accusations. I'd never heard of Santa Luisa."

Sam thought of Tiger's reference to the spice trade in the Windward Islands and the phone call he'd made to his office. If Ali was lying, he'd know soon enough.

Sam stood, rubbing at the cramp in his thigh from hours on the floor. "I have a strong feeling that this letter is the most important clue we'll ever have."

"Sam, there's nothing in there that even hints at what he did with the money."

"Nothing overt, but if we go there, I'm convinced that we'll find out what happened. We'll need to retrace his steps, do what he did. You and I are the only people who have seen this letter." He couldn't keep the excitement out of his voice. The answer was in the letter, which no one else knew about. Now he was glad she had never told the authorities.

"I have absolutely no plans to go anywhere with you, especially Santa Luisa," Ali said flatly.

"Then I'll go on my own," he announced. "I really have a feeling about this, Ali."

"How much are you being paid by Westfield?"

The question surprised him. "Enough," he said warily. "Plus a percentage when I find the money. Why?"

The look she gave him was cool and suspicious. "But not as much as if you found the money on your own and conveniently forgot to tell anyone."

"I wouldn't do that."

"I'm supposed to trust you?" she asked sarcastically. "Trust a man who couldn't tell the truth if it was staring him in the face. Maybe you're working a scam."

Sam couldn't bite back his angry words. "I lied my way on this island, but I don't intend to lie my way off."

Her expression told him she wasn't convinced. "You could use the letter, find the money and disappear, and I'd be no better off than I am now."

Sam leaned down with his hands on the arms of her chair and looked her squarely in the eye. "You have just made a case for coming with me, Ali," he said with a smile.

She squirmed inwardly but managed to stay calm under his gaze.

"Yes, come with me, and that way you can keep an eye on the detective in whom you have so little trust." He stood then.

Ali relaxed a little. "I just wish this would all go away," she said. "But it won't, not as long as you're around stirring things up."

"I'm only the messenger, Ali. It started with Casey."

She tried to give him a frigid look but he didn't buy it. "I can make arrangements for our flight and hotel—"

She held up a warning hand. "I didn't say I'd go. I need to talk with Tiger and Gwen first."

"I understand, but I can begin to work on the reservations." This time he acknowledged her disdainful look. "Separate rooms, of course."

"How about separate flights?" She took the letter from him. "I'll hold on to this. You can have it back when, and if, I decide to go with you."

7

"ARE YOU PLANNING to memorize that guidebook?"

Ali turned to Sam and regarded him with what she hoped was cool-eyed disdain. "One of us should know something about Santa Luisa." She put her glasses on top of her head.

"You've had your nose stuck in it for the whole flight."

She closed the book and put it in her carryall. He was right. Ali had rigorously disciplined herself to read the guidebook and try to ignore Sam Cantrell, who was too close for comfort in the narrow airline seat beside her. But he was impossible to ignore with his long legs stretched out onto her side, his thigh rubbing more often than necessary against hers and their shoulders, elbows, forearms constantly touching.

There was nothing she could do about their proximity, but it kept her on edge. *He* kept her on edge. No matter how she tried to ignore the memories, they remained. Ali and Sam in bed, intimate, intense.

Ali sighed. Traveling to Santa Luisa with Sam wasn't going to be easy. All she could do was try to make the best of it.

"So," he said, stretching out even farther onto her side, "what did you learn about our destination?"

"The usual. Beautiful beaches, great hotels, duty-free shops—and groves of nutmeg trees."

"Oh, yeah? The Spices of Life?"

"Could be."

Sam stayed cool. "Tell me, Ali, does Spice of Life do business on Santa Luisa?"

She heard a sharpness in his question that made her turn and look at him. "No. I would have told you if there'd been a connection. But Tiger wants me to check out the major spice sources." His expression was bland, but she saw a glimmer of intent interest in his eyes. "So I'll be doing some business while we're here, I hope, especially if I can get a good deal on nutmeg and mace."

"Not the kind you spray on attackers?"

"No," she answered, not responding to the joke.

"Well, that should be interesting, finding a new supplier for the company while we're searching out clues from Casey's letter."

"There's no reason why I shouldn't take advantage of the location," Ali replied somewhat irritably.

After that she only responded monosyllabically to Sam's questions and not at all to his remarks. Having put the guidebook aside, she gazed out the window. Far below in the turquoise Caribbean she saw the outline of a cool green island ringed by white sandy beaches. They were almost there. Her heart beat a little faster in anticipation.

After giving up on conversation, Sam watched Ali out of the corner of his eye, wondering about Spice of Life's connection—and possibly Ali's connection—to Santa

Luisa. She had denied it, but maybe there was something; maybe not. He'd find out sooner or later. In the meantime, he would retrace Casey's footsteps, which possibly would intersect with Ali's.

They were silent as the airline attendant gave instructions to prepare for landing. But Sam couldn't contain himself. He was determined to talk to her even if she responded coolly.

"I'm surprised you came," he said as he fastened his seat belt.

"So am I." Ali tried to move away from him, unsuccessfully. He seemed to take up both seats as he got ready for landing.

"I guess Tiger and Gwen thought it would be a good idea."

"No," she replied, "this was my decision. Gwen felt she'd given me enough bad advice to last a lifetime," she added sarcastically. "As for Tiger, well, being a lawyer, he laid out the facts for me, pro and con." She couldn't resist a quirky smile. "And of course he checked you out."

"I guess I'm not really surprised."

"Tiger has contacts in Atlanta. So he decided to find out what made Westfield hire you."

"Just crazy, I guess," Sam said with mock humility.

"He looked into your company, Cantrell and Greenberg—"

"Greenfield," Sam corrected.

"And discovered it was a pretty successful private-investigating firm."

"We do okay," Sam said with a twinkle in his eye.

"Then he talked to an old pal at the police department."

Sam stretched out even farther and relaxed. "My reputation with the police is pretty solid," he said.

"Apparently. You got a medal of some kind when you left the department."

"Surprised?"

Ali wasn't sure about the answer to that question. Everything about Sam had surprised her, but by now she was getting used to surprises—good and bad.

"No response? Then let me ask you this. Why did you come with me?"

She thought about that. "For two reasons. No, three," she corrected. "First, to see if Casey's letter really might hold a clue that would clear up this mess once and for all. Next, to take care of business for Spice of Life."

"As per Tiger's request?"

"Exactly."

He let that go, not pressing her further. "And your third reason?"

"To keep my eye on you."

Sam rubbed his chin thoughtfully. This was going to be an interesting trip. He wanted to trust Ali, to believe in her. And yet the cop in him had nagging doubts. It looked as if she had similar doubts about him.

It wasn't a case of the cat watching the canary. What was going on between him and Ali was the cat watching the cat. And what made it interesting was that one of the felines was male, the other female.

SAM OPENED THE DOOR to his balcony and stepped outside. The afternoon sun slanted through coconut palms and shimmered off the surface of the kidney-shaped swimming pool below. The Jacaranda Inn was nestled on a secluded cove a mile or two outside Santa Luisa's capital, the only real city on the island.

Sam was comfortable in the hotel with its two wings constructed of a pinkish gray coral. It was shaded by the fabled trees for which the hotel was named. He was a little disappointed that they weren't in bloom, more for Ali's sake than his own. The trees were most beautiful in the spring when the lavender blue flowers blossomed in clusters on bare limbs before the leaves appeared. There were jacaranda postcards everywhere, but at this time in the summer the flowers were long gone.

Still, Santa Luisa could be called a romantic island paradise, Sam thought. "But a lot of good it's doing me," he muttered as he went down the balcony stairs to Ali's patio on the ground floor.

It was empty. Sam sank into a comfortable chair and prepared to wait. Their plan was to start examining the clues in Casey's letter right away. Sam, impatient, already had checked out the hotel. It hadn't taken long for him to follow up on the police groundwork, take it a step farther and come up empty. He was a pro; the Jacaranda Inn had nothing to offer.

Having taken care of his detective mode for the moment, Sam had shifted into his Ali mode. He found that equally perplexing.

Just then she walked out the patio door. She had changed into a bright pink-and-yellow sundress, and her dark hair was piled on her head and caught up with a barrette. A few tendrils curled along her neck. She looked cool, crisp and beautiful, slightly aloof and maybe a little sad, Sam thought.

"Beautiful," Sam said, talking about Ali.

"Yes," she echoed, responding about the weather. "It's less humid here than Indigo. And there's a lovely breeze."

He nodded. "Thanks to the trade winds. All this great weather to enjoy, and we have the resort almost to ourselves."

"I guess most people vacation in the Caribbean in the winter." She sat in the chaise next to him. "Like Casey. Although we can hardly call his little sojourn here a vacation." Her voice was bitter.

"I'm in his room," Sam told her.

Ali looked at him in surprise.

"Yes. I checked it out. The room he stayed in was free. I booked it. And booked you in the one below. Do you mind?"

Ali shrugged. "You're in the room. I'm not. What do you expect to find after all this time—money hidden in the wall or under the mattress?"

Sam laughed. "No, that's not why I'm there. The police had the opportunity to search his room, and a lot of time has passed."

"Then why?"

"I don't know. A detective's eccentricity, I guess. I'm interested in setting the mood, getting a feeling for the place Casey hid out."

"I wonder why he picked a hotel like the Jacaranda Inn—a big public resort that's packed with tourists during the Christmas holidays."

"That's the answer," Sam said. "Hide in plain sight. He was just another tourist enjoying the fashionable season. There were lots of festivities going on, and it was easy for Casey—or Allen Riley—to disappear in the crowd. You still don't know any reason why he chose that name?"

"I've thought and thought about it and come up with nothing. I've also wondered why this island, why Santa Luisa?"

Her question was so innocent that Sam was thrown off for a moment. She either knew the answer or she didn't. "Why do you think?" he finally asked. Maybe she'd reverse her earlier response and reveal now that her family had dealings with the spice business on the island of Santa Luisa, and that Casey was aware of that connection, probably even used it.

"I don't have any idea."

He decided to proceed as if she were telling the truth. He wanted to believe she was. "Could be the location. The last of the Windwards, not far at all from South America, a quick plane ride to Montevideo or Rio de Janeiro."

"Or even a boat ride to the coast of, say, Colombia?"

"Right. He might have planned to bribe a fisherman from one of the villages to take him over," Sam suggested, pleased that Ali seemed to be in an investigative mood.

"South America," Ali mused. "That makes sense. Of course he'd choose a country that wouldn't extradite him back to the States while he waited for things to cool down."

"I think we're right in speculating that when the cool down came, he'd return to Santa Luisa—with you."

"And now I'm here. In the place where he died."

"I'm sure it's painful," Sam said.

She didn't seem to hear him. "It could have happened right out there." She gazed past the pool and cabanas to the turquoise Caribbean.

Sam sneaked a look at her profile. Her chin was firm, her eyes unblinking. If she was upset, she was hiding it very well. "And how does that make you feel?" he asked.

"I finished grieving for Casey a long time ago. Being here, where he died, gives a completion to my grief."

"Then it's over for you?"

"No," Ali said. "The pain won't end until we find the money." She took a deep, shaky breath. "I guess we start the search now."

"It begins with the letter." He pulled the pages from his pocket. "I've done a little preliminary footwork."

Ali was surprised that he was moving so fast. Then she remembered that Sam was the pro.

"No one recalls anything about him until the accident. Even then it took a while to connect Casey with Allen Riley."

Ali had hoped for more. "That's it?"

Sam sat back and brought her up to date. "That's all from the police report. I haven't been able to jog anything else from the memories of the staff that were here when it happened. The Jacaranda is a great place to vacation, but it's a dead end for clues."

Ali reached for the letter. "Then we have to look elsewhere." Her eyes skimmed the pages, which she almost knew by memory now. "He mentions restaurants and shops, a museum and of course the church. How do we go about this?"

"By taking our time."

"Sam—"

"Trust me, Ali. We need to get the lay of the land first, the feel of the place, before we get down to specifics. That's the way I operate."

"Except that you checked out the Jacaranda pretty quickly."

"It was a cinch. All I had to do was verify the authorities' conclusions. But the letter is another matter. No one has ever seen it but us. All the clues are here. But we have to start out slowly—together. I hope."

Ali didn't seem to have any choice. "Why not? I'll get my handbag." She stood. "Did you find out about renting a car?"

"Yep. It's waiting in the parking lot."

Again he was ahead of her. "You're a pro." She said it aloud this time.

"I hope that helps," he replied modestly.

ALI WAS GRATEFUL that the city of Avila, named for its mother city in Spain, was no more than three blocks square. She was willing to go slowly, as Sam suggested, getting a feel for the place. But Ali couldn't imagine that it would take them more than a couple of days to cover every inch of the little town.

Sam parked the rental car under the shade of a palm tree, and they strolled down the main street. There was no pressure, and Ali tried to relax. It would have been easy under normal circumstances. But there was nothing normal about this investigation, conducted by the unlikely and emotionally conflicting combination of Sam and Ali.

He seemed to be taking it all in stride, and Ali decided to do the same. They walked side by side with Ali remembering the travel book aloud. "Government House is at one end—"

"I doubt if Casey paid a visit to island officials," Sam commented.

"The wharf's at the other end of the street," Ali told him. "That would be the place to soak up some of your 'atmosphere.' Maybe if we put ourselves in Casey's shoes and try to imagine what he'd do or where he'd go..." Her voice drifted off. Sam followed her down the cobblestoned street.

"You're the one who'd know. You were married to him."

Ali flashed Sam an angry look. "Sure. Right. I really knew Casey."

"Okay," Sam said mildly. "Let's try another angle. What did he like to do? Maybe that would give us a clue."

"Spend money," Ali shot back. "I'm not being flip. Spending was Casey's one hobby." She glanced at the boutiques and shops that lined the main streets and side streets. "If you want to get a feel for Santa Luisa and Casey's place in it, then go shopping."

"Okay," Sam agreed. "We'll save that for tomorrow, and we'll show his photo."

"Don't you think the police did that already?"

"Yep. I know they did, but we'll do it again. And we have an advantage the police lacked. We know the places he frequented, the places he mentions in his letter. The police didn't have any idea where Casey spent his time. They had to put equal emphasis everywhere. We can be choosy."

They walked the entire length of the street and reached the wharf. Ali moved ahead of Sam and looked out over the fishing boats that bobbed in the harbor. Dark-skinned women sitting under umbrellas sold their wares—bananas, papayas, yams, plantains and spices to the scattering of passersby.

"Yum," Ali said. "Smell the fresh nutmeg. Most of it's supplied by one plantation. I made an appointment to see the owner tomorrow morning."

"Talk about my moving fast. We've barely just arrived and already you've found out who the major spice grower is."

"That's my line. Detecting is yours. Oh, look at those papayas. Let's take some back to the hotel to have with breakfast."

Ali chatted with the woman at the stand as she chose the fruit. Sam stood by and let her do her thing, reaching for his wallet when it was time to pay, but even then he was too slow for Ali. She bought the fruit and moved on along the rows of colorful stands. Sam followed her.

"Don't you imagine the hotel has plenty of fruit on the menu?"

Ali answered over her shoulder. "I like the idea of choosing my own. Look at these mangoes...."

By the time they reached the end of the row Ali had a complete supply of fruit. "This should last us a while."

Sam looked at the big bundle and began to laugh. "How long are you planning to be on Santa Luisa?"

Ali found herself laughing, too. It was friendly laughter, a breakthrough in their strained relationship, Sam thought. Or at least he hoped.

"Remember," she told him, "I've depended on Loomis and what we grow on Indigo. I haven't seen produce like this in ages."

Sam was thoughtful. "That's interesting. You're a prisoner on one island and a carefree, well, almost carefree tourist on this one."

"No one here knows who I am, and that's the difference."

"People forget, Ali."

She stopped and gazed up at him. "Let's concentrate on Casey and the money and not try to analyze me."

Sam sighed inwardly. The companionable moment was gone.

Ali didn't seem to have noticed. She was skimming through the letter. "Let's look for the restaurant Casey liked so much. The Blue Parrot. I think it's on a side street back this way."

"And near the church," Sam said as they hurried along.

THEY CAME UPON THE CHURCH first.

"All Saints," Sam said. He read the brass plaque on the gate. "Built in 1770. I imagine the church reflects the history of the island. You're the expert, Ali. What *is* its history?"

"Checkered. Columbus discovered Santa Luisa on one of his later voyages. Then the French fought the Spanish for it, and then the English fought the French. . . ."

Sam was watching Ali more than he was listening to her. She was looking up at the church as she talked, and the long slim line of her neck fascinated him. He let his eyes roam down the smooth, sleek skin of her back in the low-cut sundress.

"Sam . . ." She turned to look at him.

"Yes. The English fought the French," he repeated with a grin to show he had been paying attention.

"Finally Santa Luisa ended up in the British Commonwealth. British immigrants joined the Spanish and

French, and in the 1950s Santa Luisa became independent, with strong ties to England."

"Very nice and succinct, professor," he teased.

As they climbed the steps to the church Sam let himself wonder what it would be like if they were an ordinary couple, vacationing on Santa Luisa. Happy lovers, delighting in each other's company, exploring, sharing. Just being together. He felt a deep stab of loneliness. He'd blown it with Ali, and now all he could do was hope for more of those moments of laughter and togetherness, hope they would all blend together and make them a couple again.

"In the years since 1770 there must have been lots of weddings," Sam mused. "And baptisms."

"Funerals, too," Ali said, bringing him out of the romantic mood.

Once inside, Sam watched as Ali moved through the sanctuary, stopping to examine the statues and stained-glass windows. When she had made her tour of the church she returned to where he waited. "You're not interested?"

"Yes, I am. I'm interested in Casey's interest. I understand that he liked pomp and ceremony, and certainly there was plenty of that at Christmastime. But I wonder if there could have been another reason for his visits to All Saints."

Ali creased her brow and looked at Sam intently. "Do you think the church was somehow involved with the stolen money?"

Sam sat in the back pew of the church. "It's a holy place, and one where criminals sometimes seek sanctuary. Maybe it could be a hiding place, as well."

"Sam . . ."

"I'm just thinking aloud, Ali. Casey had money, lots of it. What were his choices? He could have given it to someone to keep until he could retrieve it. . . ."

"Not very likely. Casey didn't have anyone he could trust that much."

"Except you," Sam said.

"Are you doubting me again, Sam?"

"No. I'm just thinking. Another choice would have been to hide the money where it would be safe."

"Like in a church."

"But there's always someone around." As Sam spoke, a musical chord was struck, and they looked up to see a slim young man at the huge pipe organ. In the back of the church a priest blessed himself with the holy water and moved toward the altar. "No way to hide half a million dollars during the day. Maybe at night."

Quietly Sam and Ali exited out the side door into a small lush garden, rife with tropical flowers. She looked over the wrought-iron fence into the graveyard behind the church. "Maybe . . ."

"Nope," Sam answered quickly. "From what I know of your husband, he doesn't seem the kind to dig up a grave in the dead of night to hide money. That's a little too gothic for him."

Ali agreed.

"My children, may I be of assistance to you?"

Ali and Sam turned to see a plump, robust but very elderly man in clerical collar trimming the roses.

"No, Father," Ali said. "We're just exploring tourists."

The priest nodded. "Then welcome to All Saints. I'm Pat Anderson. Father Pat to my parishioners."

They exchanged handshakes. "You're British?" Ali asked.

"Irish, actually. A holdover from another time. I survived the island's independence, and for some reason they decided to keep me on."

"It's a wonderful place for a parish," Ali observed.

"Heavenly, you might almost say," Father Pat retorted.

Sam spoke for the first time. "To tell you the truth, Father, we're here investigating a crime."

The priest put his pruning shears aside. "That would be the Allen Riley case?"

"How did you know?"

The old priest laughed. "We experience petty theft occasionally on Santa Luisa, even here at All Saints, but nothing in the realm of half a million dollars. That was significant."

Father Pat joined Ali and Sam, who were seated on one of the marble benches in the garden. "It's been the talk of the island all this time."

"I suppose you told the police everything you knew," Sam said.

"In fact, they never came to see me."

Ali was surprised, but not Sam.

"And for a long time I didn't know who Allen Riley was. Then I realized I'd seen him in my congregation."

"But you didn't alert the police?" Ali asked.

"There was nothing to tell them." Father Pat sat beside them on the bench. "He was here once or twice during the Christmas season."

"But you never had any personal contact with him?" Sam asked.

Father Pat shook his head. "He always slipped out before the recessional. And I don't have to tell you, he never came to confession. Something tells me that Allen Riley simply loved the grandeur of our holiday services."

"Father, do you think it's possible he could have hidden all that money in the church?" Ali asked.

Father Pat shook his head. "As you see, there is always someone here."

"But at night?"

"Unfortunately, the petty theft I refer to has necessitated that we keep the church and the grounds locked at night."

SAM AND ALI CONTINUED their climb up the hill, leaving the church behind. He took her arm and was gratified that she didn't pull away.

"I think we can safely say the money's not hidden in Father Pat's church," Sam said.

"I'll second that observation," Ali said. She was beginning to accept the fact that they were a team. "But that means we've hit another dead end."

"Don't worry. We're just beginning."

"Well, I don't expect we'll find any hidden secrets in the Blue Parrot."

"But it looks appealing, doesn't it?" he asked as they approached the bar.

"It's everything a tropical bar should be."

Inside, the Blue Parrot was dark and paneled in a deep tropical mahogany. A parrot in a cage at the door squawked a threatening hello and a few other remarks, most of them expletives.

Double doors led to a small, intimate courtyard where Ali and Sam found a table nestled among palms and hibiscus. A cooling fountain splashed in the center of the courtyard. The sun was setting, and there was a heady, sensual fragrance of summer flowers on the twilight air.

They ordered the house special, rum punch, and then sat back to savor the quiet. There were a few customers in the bar, but they had the garden setting to themselves.

Ali took a long sip of her drink. "That hits the spot. Detecting is thirsty work, but I guess you know that."

"I've been at it a while. But where this job is concerned, there's nothing here to detect, so let's just enjoy the scene."

"That suits me," Ali said. "No Casey talk. But how about some Sam talk? What can you tell me about yourself as a detective?"

"Not much," he replied.

Ali thoughtfully studied Sam through narrowed eyes. "I have a theory about you," she said.

"Uh-oh." He sounded wary but was in fact curious and pleased that Ali had spent any time thinking about him.

"You've chosen the perfect career for yourself."

"That's the theory?"

"Yep. Shall I explain?"

"Please," he said.

"Even after your confession about being a private detective and ex-policeman, I still don't know anything about you."

"Well, you know—"

"Oh, I know you can be charming and smooth."

"Not much of a recommendation," Sam observed.

"And you're intelligent, and of course very adept at playing roles."

"Comes in handy," he admitted.

"But you don't like to reveal anything about yourself, and so you've chosen the perfect career."

"I'm still not quite with you."

"Then listen to this, Sam Cantrell. You can spy and ask questions and investigate—and still keep yourself hidden away."

"I didn't know I was so transparent."

"You're not. I've taken a lot of time to figure you out, to discover how secretive you are."

Sam sipped his drink and looked across at Ali. "And yet you're the expert on hiding out," he told her finally.

"Touché, Sam. A nice little barb."

"I didn't mean it to be a barb. It's the truth. You've spent the last two years hiding." Her mouth tightened and her shoulders tensed. He could tell he'd touched a nerve with her. But he didn't back away. "Maybe that will change," he said.

"If we find the money it will, but so far we haven't made much headway," she said ruefully.

"We've only been here a day, Ali, long enough to find out that the money isn't hidden at the hotel or the church."

"Or this bar."

"Before we leave I'll talk to the bartender and show him Casey's photo, but I expect you're right. The Blue Parrot isn't going to give us a clue. However, it has something to offer, I believe. A good meal. Let's order."

An hour later, after courses of conch chowder, grilled grouper, fresh greens and citrus salad, and a dessert of mango ice cream, they ordered coffee and sat back to watch the moon rise.

"What a sumptuous meal," Ali said. "Tiger would kill for the fish recipe. In fact, he'd like all these exotic choices on the menu."

"Maybe you should talk to the chef."

"I might do that," she teased. "You check out the bartender about Casey, and I'll do the tourist thing."

"Casey was a good tourist himself when it came to restaurants," Sam said as he sipped the strong black coffee.

"Nothing but the best for him—good food, expensive wine. Maître d's loved to see us coming in Atlanta. Casey tipped everyone in sight."

"Did that bother you?"

Ali started to answer and then changed her mind. "No more about me, Sam. You know enough of how Casey and I lived in Atlanta. Big house, fine restaurants—as if we had money," she added wryly. "Now what about you? Or do you only ask questions, never answer them?"

"I *can* answer. Just tell me what you want to know." Despite his easy response, Sam could feel himself tensing.

"For starters, where do you live in Atlanta?"

"In a condo on Peachtree Street."

"Hmm, nice address."

"I just bought the place. Before that I rented a furnished apartment. But business has been good recently—"

She smiled sweetly. "And will be even better if we find the money."

"*When* we find it," he corrected.

"Did you enjoy furnishing your new condo?"

Sam looked down at his cup. "Well, it's not exactly furnished. More like a bed, a table and a chair. I just haven't had the time."

Ali nodded. "I get the picture, Sam. A place to sleep, shower and change clothes, but not a home. Am I right?"

"You're too damned smart, Ali. I've never had a place that I'd call home," he said slowly, truthfully.

Ali wasn't surprised as she began putting together the picture of a man who was a loner, who didn't let anyone get close, who spent his time and energy finding out about others. Against all common sense, she was becoming fascinated by him again, just as she had been that first day in the greenhouse.

"You're not married, I gather. Now or ever." Why was she asking that? She should have let well enough alone. He was a loner; let him be.

"Right again. Not now. Not ever."

"Live with someone?" There she went again, prying, showing her interest. While he hesitated over his answer, she decided to go for it since she had gotten this far. "I know the answer, Sam. You've had lots of girlfriends because you're sexy and know how to flirt and . . . make love." Obviously, she *was* going for it. "But you've never let a woman live with you, never let a woman, or anyone, intrude in your private world."

"I didn't know you were psychic," he said with a wry smile.

Ali raised an eyebrow and smiled. "Once I caught on, you weren't that hard to read."

He pushed back his chair. "Excuse me for a minute. It's time to talk to the bartender. I'll be right back."

Ali settled back in her chair and watched him through the open doors. Very prickly, Investigator Sam Cantrell, at least about his own life. Mysterious, even. She'd scared him away. But he would be back. She wondered why she was interested, but of course she knew the answer. Part of her was still holding on to Sam, and she didn't know if she could let go.

THEY DROVE BACK to the Jacaranda Inn in silence. Sam helped Ali out of the rental car and took her arm with deliberate casualness, then led her toward the beach. The full moon was beginning to wane, but it was still bright enough to cast silvery beams across the Caribbean and light their path.

The evening had gone well, Sam thought. He and Ali were friends—well, almost friends—again. She'd even gotten personal with him in her probing questions.

"How about a walk?" he suggested.

"Sorry," Ali made herself say. "I don't think so. Walking on the beach with you can be hazardous to a woman's emotions."

Sam guided her to her patio door. No point in pushing. He would just have to prove that his feelings for her had nothing to do with his investigation. Meanwhile, hands off. Not an easy command, he realized as she gazed up at him, her face luminous in the moonlight. He was reminded of another time on another island. His body ached with wanting her and remembered everything about making love to her, the scent of her hair, how she tasted, how her skin felt against his, how she moved in his arms.

If he could kiss her again and hold her then maybe everything would be all right. Maybe he wouldn't have to wait until he could prove himself. He touched her face with the tips of his fingers. "Ali, I—"

She stepped away. "No, Sam. It's not going to happen again. No more moonlight kisses and all that follows. I meant everything I told you back on Indigo. This isn't about you and me. It's about Casey and the damned half a million dollars."

"This is crazy," he blurted out. "I care about you, Ali, and I think you care about me. I know you do," he challenged. "Whatever was between us hasn't vanished. We still both feel it."

"No!" Her answer was a sharp, almost desperate denial.

"Ali—"

"No," she cried again. "I'm not going to fall in love with you, Sam. I won't let that happen." She whirled and moved away from him across the patio.

Sam heard her fumble with the door and then saw her vanish into the room.

Fall in love.

He took a deep, shaky breath. Love. That's what it was all about. And it was scary as hell.

8

THE PHONE CALL Sam had waited for on Indigo hadn't
come so he decided it was time to take action. He got up
early and put in a long-distance call to his partner in Atlanta.

Two minutes into the conversation Sam was smiling.
"So there's nothing to connect Ali or Spice of Life to any
of the brokers down here. How about Casey?"

Sam listened for a minute more to Jerry's assurances
that the Casey Bell spice connection was a dead end.
Then he hung up, expressing his thanks to Jerry but
keeping his relief to himself. His partner didn't need to
know everything.

LATER THAT MORNING Ali and Sam drove along the coast
road north of the city. Ali had made an appointment with
the largest nutmeg grower on the island, and when she'd
expressed her concern about negotiating the unfamiliar
Santa Luisa roads, Sam had offered to drive her to the
plantation.

Steep cliffs dropped off to the turquoise blue Caribbean far below. On the other side of the narrow road
gently rolling green hills rose toward the mountains that
bisected Santa Luisa. A little fearful of heights, Ali was

glad to be in the passenger seat, close to the hills and away from the sheer drop.

She carefully studied the road signs and the map supplied by the rental car company, deliberately pretending to be engrossed. Last night's scene with Sam was still haunting her. She'd told him point-blank that she wasn't going to fall in love with him, but why the hell had she even mentioned love?

Unless it was very much on her mind.

So far, Sam hadn't alluded to the conversation of the night before, probably because he was just as confused as Ali by her behavior. There was no explaining her feelings about Sam, even to herself. No need to try. She sighed and fixed her attention on the road.

As Ali studied the map, Sam sneaked his own look— at Ali. She was wearing shorts, and just the glimpse of her long tanned legs and the scent of her perfume floating on the air made all his nighttime fantasies come vividly alive.

Earlier, he had wished he could stop wanting her. Now he knew that was never going to happen. He forced his eyes back to the road. He had to stay alert; the curves were dangerous, and he could sense Ali's nervousness. But her curves were dangerous, too, Sam thought with a secret smile.

The road veered away from the sea, to Ali's relief. She studied the map again. "I think we're on the right track. The next turnoff should lead to the spice plantation."

"Not much traffic to contend with." The road flattened out and stretched emptily ahead of them. In fact, they hadn't met a car, and Sam's comment was only an attempt to keep up the conversation. All kinds of feelings were churning inside, and yet he knew Ali was less than receptive.

The thaw that had begun between them the night before had cooled to careful politeness. Sam wanted to confront Ali with her remark about falling in love. Hell, she was probably as scared of the idea as he. But now that the words were said, they couldn't be taken back. It was time for them to confront the subject of love.

Yet whenever he tried to talk to her, the conversation always ended badly. Disastrously, in fact, with Ali fleeing from him.

He glanced at her profile, cool and unapproachable, and tried another innocuous comment. "Nice scenery along this stretch of road."

To his surprise, that generated a response. "It's beautiful, and it leads right to those houses in the hills. You can catch a glimpse of a tiled roof now and then or a turret. Look, Sam, there're miles of fences and rock walls. The estates must be huge."

"That's another side of Santa Luisa," Sam commented. "They're probably empty until the season begins in December." Sam was thoughtful for a long while as he drove. There was wealth in the hills. Could Casey have had access to the owners of the estates? It was a question for later, he decided.

"Is that the turnoff ahead?" he asked.

"I think so."

"You think so? You're the navigator," he said in jest.

Ali's response surprised him. "You didn't have to come with me," she snapped. "I could have handled my business alone."

"Ali, I was kidding."

"But I guess you wanted to keep tabs on me."

Sam clamped his lips together and hung a hard right onto the road that snaked through rows of giant flowering poinciana trees. "I thought I was doing you a favor," he said, "coming along on this trip as your driver."

After a long pause Ali admitted, "Well, it *was* a relief not to have to drive along that treacherous road. So in that way you did me a favor. Sorry, I guess I'm a little tense about the meeting this morning."

Sam bit back his response. Ali was tense about the whole damned trip. Obviously this wasn't the time to bring up what had happened between them last night. He kept his mouth shut, and they drove in silence to the nutmeg plantation.

They were met by Mr. Aguilla, a native of the island, whose family had for aeons farmed the land that was now his spice plantation.

"We're originals, I guess, after the Indians whose tribes settled here and then died out. We keep on going. Some of my workers have been with me for thirty years," Aguilla boasted. "We're all growing old together, including my trees which can last sixty years. They aren't native to the West Indies, but they do very well here."

He led them to the processing shed where he picked a nutmeg from one of the trays and pulled it apart. There was a network of orange fibers around the seed, which he showed to them.

"It looks almost like lace," Ali said.

"That's the mace. We dry and process it separately. The kernel inside is the nutmeg."

"You do everything here?" Ali asked.

"Oh, yes. We grow the plant, harvest it, separate out the mace and nutmeg, dry, grind, pack and ship. No fancy packaging for grocery boutiques. We sell by bulk."

"That's exactly what I want," Ali said. "Can we talk business?"

SAM SAT on the wide veranda while Aguilla and Ali carried on their business inside the house. The scene was quiet and peaceful with the scent of drying nutmeg hovering in the air and the sound of voices soft and melodious from the work sheds. The whole ambience was one of heady sensuality. For the hundredth time Sam regretted that his trip to Santa Luisa had anything to do with Casey Bell and the damned money.

Aguilla and Ali celebrated their business deal with a toast. "It's sherry, Mr. Cantrell, but I expect you would like something stronger?"

"I'll learn to be a connoisseur." Sam took a sip from the glass and toasted with Ali and Aguilla.

"The lady drives quite a bargain," Aguilla complimented.

Sam agreed. "She's a fine businesswoman."

"She will send me samples of the Spice of Life line, which I am sure can be placed in island stores," Aguilla said. "Gourmet foods are very popular here. During the season Santa Luisa does an astounding amount of business. Our island has become a refuge for the rich and famous."

"We saw some of their homes on the way here," Sam commented.

"Huge estates built back in the hills by the wealthy from all over the world—Switzerland, France, Japan, Kuwait. They love to come to Santa Luisa, especially for Christmas."

"What do they do—the rich and famous?" Sam asked.

"They party, shop and trade. Have you been into our stores?"

"Not yet," Sam answered. He was thinking of the wealthy not as shoppers or partyers but as traders. Casey had come to Santa Luisa with money. The holiday residents might well have had something to trade.

"You'll be astounded at what's offered here, duty free, of course. Chinaware, silver, crystal, couture clothing and jewels, the very finest...."

Sam's attention was caught by the word *jewels*. Had Casey turned the cash into a diamond? Easy to hide, he thought before dismissing the idea. The police would have tracked down a jewelry sale of half a million dollars on an island as small as Santa Luisa. Sam had read the reports; their search of banking records on the island had been thorough. But Casey could have done business on the black market, making a private deal. Sam's detective mind was having a field day.

Aguilla followed them to the car, still spouting his spice knowledge. "You know, my dear," he said to Ali, "I have just remembered where I heard the name before."

"Spice of Life?"

"Yes, it was in a telephone call I received from a gentleman in Atlanta, Georgia, of all places, asking if I had ever done business with Spice of Life or a man called Casey Bell. Of course, the answer was no at the time. Not until we signed our contracts did I realize that Ali Paxton was connected to Spice of Life. Isn't that an odd coincidence?"

"Yes, it is." It was Sam who answered; he had no choice. He knew Ali wasn't going to respond. He had seen her jaw tighten just before she flashed him a look of pure contempt.

Sam was relieved that Aguilla seemed oblivious to the building fireworks as he thanked Ali for her order and bade them a friendly goodbye.

Ali gave Aguilla a firm handshake, murmured a few words of thanks and climbed into the car, her shoulders stiff and tight.

She waited until they rounded the first curve in the road. "You'd better stop this car right now, Sam Cantrell."

He kept on driving. "Why? We can talk while we're driving."

"Not if I'm attacking you with everything I have."

Sam glanced over at her. "You mean your handbag?"

Ali gritted her teeth. "You lied to me again," she accused. "You lied and manipulated me. You were the one who was checking up on me, weren't you? I just can't figure out what the hell you wanted to know."

Sam stopped the car under the shade of a tree and quickly held up his hands. "Don't attack until I explain."

"There're no excuses left, Sam."

"I'm not looking for excuses. I had to know if Casey came to Santa Luisa because of its special ties to Spice of Life or if it was pure coincidence."

"There were no ties to Spice of Life."

"I know that now, Ali."

"You knew it before, Sam. The truth is, I'd never heard of this damned island until Casey turned up here. I told you that. The problem is, you didn't believe me."

"As a man, as your lover, I believed you." He tried not to notice her wince at his words. "As a professional investigator, I had to be sure."

"Did you think Aguilla had laundered money for Casey? Or hidden him? Or flown him to Bolivia? Do you think everyone has an angle?"

The questions came one upon the other, without allowing Sam time to respond. He waited, his mouth set in a stubborn line. "I'm not going to apologize, Ali," he said finally. "I'm only sorry you had to find out from Aguilla, and I realize now he was a blind alley."

"That seems to be your way, Sam. You always wait a little too long to clue me in. What other secrets do you have?"

"None," he said adamantly.

Ali let her head fall back against the seat, eyes closed. "Last night I felt it happening again. I felt you getting to me, just like on Indigo. I was so close . . . so close to letting you in." She sat upright and looked at him with angry eyes. "Thank God I didn't! Won't I ever learn?"

Sam started the engine. "Maybe I'm the one who ought to learn." The car bolted forward. "No matter what I do or say, you read something sinister into it." He pulled out onto the road. "The truth is, and always has been, that I was hired to find the damned money—and then I met you."

"And decided to use me." Her words were bitter.

He stopped the car again.

"Are you going to keep stopping and starting over and over?" she snapped.

"Maybe. If you keep arguing with me."

"Then let me out."

"Get out. I'm not stopping you. It's a long walk along a deserted road back to the hotel."

Ali opened the door, hesitated at his words and then got out anyway, slamming the door after her.

Sam got out on his side and followed. He caught up with Ali under the trees and grabbed her arm.

"I made some other decisions, too," he said. "I decided that you were the sexiest, most exciting woman I'd ever met. And the most mixed up."

She turned to face him, pulling her arm away. "Mixed up? Because I didn't trust you? Because you lied to me on a regular basis?"

"I didn't lie. Sometimes I just delayed the truth a little," he equivocated.

"Expediency instead of honor. Is that your motto, Sam?"

He took a deep breath. "I know you don't trust me, Ali."

"I don't trust *you?* Ha! You had your partner check up on *me*, Sam."

"You had Tiger call Atlanta about *me*."

At a momentary impasse, they glared at each other. Then Sam tore his eyes away from hers.

"Jerry said there wasn't a connection between Casey and the spice dealers. I realize you had nothing to do with his stealing the money. So let it go, Ali. It's not even an issue now."

"Oh?" It was a cold, solitary little word.

He took the opportunity to grab her arm again and head her in the direction of the car. "It's not going to do you any good to be flailing around out here in the wilderness."

"I'm not flailing around," she argued, but she let herself be led back to the car.

"Trust is hard to rebuild after what you went through with Casey. You say you don't trust me, but I don't think you trust yourself. If you did, you'd stop fighting me and we could work on this together."

"Together? That's strange coming from you," Ali said as she allowed Sam to open the car door and help her inside. Then she waited until he got in before attacking again.

"Look at your life, Sam. You're a loner. You don't know how to be with another person. You don't have a clue about togetherness."

Ali saw his knuckles turn white as he gripped the steering wheel, and she knew her words had hit home. She was glad. She had lashed out blindly, wanting to hurt him, and she'd succeeded.

"Are you trying to drive me crazy, Ali?"

"I could ask you the same thing."

"I've never known a woman like you."

"Ditto," she said. "Furthermore, I haven't had a decent night's sleep since—"

"Since we met?"

"No," she said shakily.

"Since we made love?"

"No!" she repeated.

"Since when, Ali?"

"Never mind," she said. "I don't want to discuss it."

"You brought it up."

She had been thinking about all the sleepless nights since they'd met, but there was no way she'd let him know how many nights there'd been. "Anyway, you make me crazy, too, so I think we should work independently from now on." She glanced at him sharply. "Unless you still don't trust me alone."

"That was a mistake," Sam said as he pulled the car back onto the road. "I know now that you had nothing to do with Casey and the money. I've felt that all along, but I had to have it verified factually. Besides, I thought you wanted to keep your eyes on *me*."

"Nope, not anymore. If you found the money, you wouldn't run with it. You'd want all the glory and glamour—and the reward. You'd want to be proven right. Just think of the great newspaper coverage."

"If I do find the money, you'll be the first to know."

"Good. Now that we both trust each other—" her voice was heavy with sarcasm "—we can get to work. I'll take the shops on one side of Main Street and you can have the other. We'll meet back at the Jacaranda tonight and compare notes. Or at least I'll share what I've found out."

"So will I," he repeated wearily. "I don't have any more secrets."

"I'll bet."

"But I think we should stick together, Ali. I think—"

"No, I need to be alone, Sam. I can ask questions about Casey as well as you."

"All right," Sam agreed wearily. They rode in silence until the outskirts of the town came into view. "Double-check the jewelry shops. I know the police investigated them, but . . ."

Ali smiled sweetly, but her voice had the prickle of thorns in it. "If jewelry is a big commodity on Santa Luisa, maybe Casey tried to convert the money. I saw the glazed look in your eyes when Aguilla mentioned the big-time spenders up in the hills."

Sam gave her a quick grin. "You drive me crazy, Ali, but you're damned smart. If Casey didn't stash the money, then he must have converted it. I'll check with

Government House and find out who owns those big estates. There could be a tie-in."

"Then we'll meet at the Jacaranda."

When Sam slowed at an intersection Ali opened the door.

"Maybe we should meet at the car," he argued, "and drive back together."

Ali shook her head. "No, I'll get a taxi. The team of Cantrell and Paxton, if it ever existed, is out of business."

"Ali—"

She got out of the car. "Don't wait up for me, Sam. I may be late."

SAM WAS SITTING on her patio when Ali returned from town. "Just wanted to be sure you got home okay."

She flashed him a withering look. "Getting around in Santa Luisa is pretty simple, even for an amateur detective." She flopped into a chair and gazed out over the Caribbean where remnants of a brilliant sunset lingered. "I didn't find out a damned thing except that Santa Luisa has some great shops. If I was a conspicuous consumer I'd have shopping bags filled with purchases. They're pushing Christmas gifts already."

"I noticed. I don't know how many times a clerk wanted to sell me perfume or a sexy nightgown or jewelry for the special woman in my life." His mouth turned down in a wry grimace at the phrase. "Duty free, of course, and gift wrapped for Christmas."

"Except Christmas isn't your thing, or mine," Ali reminded him. "Did you learn anything about Casey or the money?"

"Not much. Tomorrow a clerk at Government House will have some information on the owners of those estates up in the hills. There's an outside chance one of them will have a connection with Casey."

"An outside chance?"

"Frankly, I'm not too hopeful, Ali."

"Most of the salespeople I talked with said the Christmas season is so busy they can't pay attention to any one customer. Of course, they would remember someone who spent half a million."

Sam nodded tiredly. "I'm convinced he spent it but obviously not in a shop. He purchased something worth a hell of a lot of money."

"And then?"

"Either he got it out of the country . . ."

"Or he didn't."

Sam smiled wryly. "Those are our choices."

Ali sighed.

"We can go over the letter again tonight, analyze it once more."

"I guess. Though I wonder what good it will do. I understand now why you checked up on the spice dealers, Sam. You were reaching for a clue, any clue. Right now I'd do the same thing. This whole operation is like looking for a needle in a haystack. I wonder . . ." She paused.

"What?"

"I wonder if we shouldn't just go home, forget all this."

"No," he said almost fiercely. "The answer's out there, and we'll find it. Besides, I'm in too deep, Ali. I can't walk away." His voice was husky with emotion. "Not from the case or from you. Especially not from you with so much unsettled between us."

"Unsettled? Nothing's unsettled, Sam. It's over. I thought we—"

"I won't accept that, Ali," he interrupted. "I'll never forget what happened between us, how it felt to make love to you, how much I want you even now."

Darkness came rushing at them, a thick, heavy tropical night, and Ali was relieved to be able to hide in it. She didn't want him to see the confusion on her face. She fought a tremor in her voice. "There was hurt, too, Sam, and anger and lies."

In the darkness he took her hand and squeezed it hard. "What I remember is the passion and the need. Does it make sense that I need you, Ali?"

"This isn't the time, Sam."

He held on to her hand. "Answer me, Ali."

"All right," she said fiercely. "It doesn't make sense that we'd be together at all! We're two people who never should have met."

"Or two people who were destined to meet."

Ali sat up in surprised silence. "I can't believe you said that." Her heart was beating faster now. She wanted to hear what he was saying, and yet she was afraid to hear it.

His reply was slow and deliberate. "I think I was meant to help you get off Indigo and back into life."

She started to protest, but he overrode her.

"And I think you were meant to hold a mirror up to me and my life. I've been thinking about what you said all day, Ali, that I don't let people in. It's true. I keep everyone at a distance. I tell myself I'm investigating when what I'm really doing is looking for excuses not to get close."

"I wasn't criticizing you, Sam. I realize that it can be frightening to get too close, to love too much." Her voice was shaky.

For a long time, he didn't speak. Then finally he said, "At least you've had love. I don't think that anyone has ever really loved me."

"Your parents, surely."

"Maybe. I really don't know. I told you about them— the drinking and fighting?"

"Yes," Ali said quietly. "But still, they *were* your parents...."

Sam let go of her hand, got up and walked over to the patio railing. He stood silently, looking out into the nearly black night, watching the whitecaps form, the only light in the darkness.

Ali stayed where she was, hoping he would come back and talk with her but not bold enough to ask him to.

Sam turned back toward her. She could barely make out the silhouette of his tall frame against the night. "My dad walked out on us, Ali. Vanished. I still don't know what happened to him, if he's dead or alive. My mom had been sick for a long time. After he left, she seemed to give up. By then she didn't care about much of anything, including me. I told you that she died just before Christmas."

"Yes, I remember," she said softly.

"I was fifteen."

"But there must have been other family?"

The sound he made, deep down in his throat, was hard and cynical, more like a snicker than a laugh. "Most of us don't have people like Tiger and Gwen waiting in the wings. Whatever family there was didn't give a damn."

He walked back and sat beside her but didn't take her hand again. "I was put into foster care where I lasted about a month. The people were nice but totally unequipped to deal with a rebellious, angry teenager. I realize now that I was more sad than angry, but whatever the feelings, I didn't know how to express them. Except by hitting out."

Ali reached for his hand, found it in the dark and held on. The gesture surprised Sam, but he didn't pull away. Instead, he clung to her warm soft hand.

"What happened?" she asked softly.

"I ran away, of course. Not a very original reaction, I admit, but my only choice, or so I thought. The streets seemed friendlier to me than anywhere else."

"Where were those streets—not in Atlanta?"

"No. I guess you can tell I didn't grow up in the old South. But I didn't tell you where I was from."

"There's a lot you didn't tell, Sam."

"Now I feel like telling it all. If you feel like listening."

"Yes," she whispered. "I do." Ali tightened her fingers around Sam's hand. She remembered the Fourth of July night on the beach when he'd taken her hand and she'd talked about Casey and the past. That had been the beginning for them.

Now everything had come full circle.

Ali leaned toward Sam, hoping she could understand the forces that pulled them together and at the same time pushed them apart.

"I grew up in Philadelphia. South Philly, which at the time was a tough place that suited me. I was a tough kid. But I wasn't particularly smart. I got picked up fairly often by the police." He was thoughtful for a while, holding her hand firmly. "When I saw those pictures of you and Casey, how you lived, the house, the pool, I thought of my own life. We came from different worlds. But I guess you noticed that about me from the first."

"I knew you were tougher than I was, Sam. I had the feeling you'd had experiences that I had never dreamed of."

He chuckled without amusement. "You've never known anyone like me."

"Sam, my husband absconded with half a million dollars! I'm not so innocent."

Sam smiled silently. "That's white-collar crime, Ali. The crime committed by privileged people who grew up in a privileged world. My world included gangs, juvenile detention halls, police cars. They were my homes. I was seventeen when my probation officer gave me a choice—jail time or army time. Back then it was standard operating procedure to give kids a way out. Naturally, I took the army. And it was my salvation. For the first time in my life I had discipline and order and rules that had to be obeyed."

Ali was beginning to understand. "The same reasons you later became a policeman."

"Exactly. When your world is crazy, you look for order wherever you can find it."

"But the story has a happy ending. You made it, Sam."

He dropped her hand suddenly and stood. "I bet you're hungry. Want some dinner?"

"Oh, no, Sam Cantrell. You're not putting me off that easily. I'll get us drinks from the minibar in my room. Remember all that fruit I bought? We can have that for dinner. You said you wanted to talk. Well, I want to listen. I'm going to hear this story all the way through."

Bemused, Sam grinned. "You love to give orders, don't you, Ali?" Before she had a chance to answer he added, "Go get your drinks and fruit. I'll talk as long as you'll listen."

9

ALI STOOD IN THE MIDDLE of her room, staring at the small refrigerator. She had already decided to mix their drinks and take the fruit out to the patio for them to share while she listened to the rest of his story. She wanted to hear it, and yet she stood confronting the minibar, not moving. Ali knew why. In listening to him she would be leaving herself open to raw feelings, deep reactions. That wouldn't be easy.

She took the first step and opened the fridge. The rest was easy, filling glasses with ice and mixing the gin and tonics, piling the fruit in a big bowl. Had it been only yesterday that she had bought the papayas and mangoes on the wharf? It seemed like a million years ago.

Ali put everything on a tray. There. She was ready to go back to Sam. She never had imagined that he would open up to her and draw her into his life, a world of darkness and danger, a place where she was a stranger. It was frightening to look inside someone else and see the pain, but she was the one who was pushing, asking that he tell her everything.

Ali took a deep breath, picked up the tray and headed for the patio. Sam pulled two chairs up to the table, and they ate in silence. Music drifted on the air from the ho-tel bar, accompanied by the occasional sound of laughter. It seemed to Ali that she and Sam were in their own little world.

"That was a good idea—to buy the fruit," he said as they finished. "Thanks."

"You're welcome." She was silent, waiting for him to pick up where he had left off. When it didn't happen she insisted. "Keep on going, Sam. Tell me why you came to Atlanta."

"Lots of reasons," he said lightly. "Because Atlanta was so green and welcoming. Because there was a graciousness in the way of life that I'd never known before. Mostly because I got a job."

Ali smiled. "And a good job. You must have been a fine policeman. You got an award."

His expression changed then. "Oh, yeah. My award. It had a high price, and I'm not sure I want to talk about that."

"You wouldn't let me run from my past, Sam." She didn't want to pressure him, but she wasn't about to lose him now.

"You're sure you want to hear this?"

"I'm sure."

"Okay." He pushed away from the table. "I was a cop a long time ago. And I loved it. I took to the authority and discipline, and I liked to help people, corny as that sounds. I was lucky enough to have a great partner, an older guy named Hank. He was my rabbi."

"Rabbi?"

"Cop talk. Like a mentor. He became the father, the brother I never had. Then one night…" He couldn't hide the quiver in his voice.

Ali was silent and motionless, careful not to do anything to distract him.

"One night on patrol we got called to a family argument, husband and wife having a fight, disturbing the neighbors, nothing unusual. They lived over a store. We parked the car, went up the outside stairs and knocked on the door. Hank was ahead of me. The guy opened the door and started shooting. It was crazy. Nothing but a family dispute, and the guy comes out shooting. He got Hank right in the gut. Then the guy tore off down the stairs. I didn't have time to call out for him to stop. We traded fire, and I got off the best shot."

"Your scar," she whispered.

He nodded. "I walked away with a nasty wound. But Hank and the other guy were dead. The shooter was a kid, Ali, only nineteen or twenty."

"But he killed your partner."

"Yeah, and I was a hero. Picture in the paper, big award. I was a great guy for shooting someone who'd had a fight with his wife."

"He was violent, Sam."

"I know. It ought to add up. Rationally, it should all work out. He was crazed, he shot my partner. He would have shot anyone who got in his way. But he needed help. He didn't need to die."

"Neither did Hank."

"No. Especially not Hank. I knew that, but it didn't matter. I still wanted out—off the police force. I kept thinking about how it could have been avoided. Neither Hank nor I were prepared for what happened, but I should have taken the call more seriously, covered Hank, I should have—"

"You were the rookie cop, Sam. It was Hank's responsibility."

"Technically. But he was a trusting kind of guy in spite of all his years on the force. Anyway, I couldn't take it after that. I knew I had to change my life or crack up."

"You quit the force."

"Yep. I had no plans, no future, but I knew I could never go back to a beat. Then Jerry came along. He had read about me in the paper. His firm specialized in solving white-collar crime, high rollers, big money, all nice and sanitized. That sounded great to me. He offered me a job. I took it and I didn't look back. I forced myself never to think of Hank again, or the kid."

"In other words, you shut everything—everyone—out?"

Sam paused a moment and looked toward Ali in the darkness. "To tell you the truth, I made a decision that money and success mattered. Nothing else. I did my job and I did it well. Made partner. Made money. Frankly, Ali, you were just another case, a woman who thought she could fool me. I knew better."

Ali didn't respond.

"I had handled a dozen cases like this with no problems. I never expected that after one day with you I'd be on an emotional roller coaster."

Sam got up, avoided looking at Ali and walked to the edge of the patio. He stood there for a long time, gazing out into the blackness. "You've brought out feelings in me that I'd buried for years. Because of you, I've relived things I thought were gone and forgotten. Like Hank and the kid. I'd buried all that. I was hiding. Just like you."

Ali felt herself wince. But there was something else. "You still carry a gun," she said softly.

"It's part of my job, part of my image, and Jerry is careful about image. Clients are, too. I doubt if I ever would use a gun again."

He was quiet, and so was Ali.

"So that's it, Ali," he said finally. "The Sam Cantrell story. Not a pretty picture."

Images flashed through her mind—Sam as a little boy craving love and getting rejection, a child alone struggling to make connection with people and losing at every turn. She felt her defenses melting.

"But it's a human story," she said. "A real one." She moved instinctively across the patio and put her arms around him. "I'm so sorry, Sam."

"I don't want your pity, Ali. That isn't why I told you." His body felt stiff and unyielding.

"This isn't pity I'm feeling," she insisted. "Sadness and regret . . ."

"That's not what I want, either," he said.

"Then what *do* you want?" She was desperate to understand what was happening between them.

"I told you about my life because I didn't want anymore secrets between us. And as for what I want, you know what that is, Ali. It's what we never talk about." He put his hands on her shoulders and gazed down at her. "Oh, if you could see your eyes in the moonlight. They give you away, Ali. I've confused and frightened you."

"Frightened? No, Sam."

The look in his eyes was cool and measuring, a look she'd seen so often. "Maybe you *should* be frightened, Ali. A man with a past like mine, a man who has killed, who doesn't know anything about love."

Ali's eyes wavered from his, and Sam dropped his hands and stepped away.

"Your past isn't what I expected. I mean—" she began, feeling the sting of unbidden tears.

"I never pretended to be Sir Galahad."

Ali struggled for the right words. "Maybe you're wounded inside, in your heart, just as I am. It isn't easy for us—"

He interrupted. "Is this the pity part again? Or the part where we talk about all the reasons this relationship won't work? The bottom line is that I'm a loner, Ali. Maybe my past should be a warning to you. Maybe I was wrong to ever think—" He broke off. "Hell, I need a drink."

Ali felt the tears building again, but she didn't want to cry in front of him. She felt inadequate and unprepared for what he'd told her. "I'll fix you another gin and tonic," she offered.

"No, I need something stronger, like a straight shot of tequila. It's not often that I spill my guts and then realize I've done the wrong thing."

"No, you haven't, Sam." She didn't know what else to say. Inwardly she ached for time alone to think about what he'd told her.

"I'm going to the hotel bar," he announced. Then as an afterthought he offered, "Want to join me?"

"No, I . . ."

His face was hard, as if carved in stone, denying any emotions. "I guess both of us need time to think. See you tomorrow." He stalked into the darkness.

Ali reached out toward his retreating back and then dropped her hand. He'd told her too much, opened himself up too completely, and now he was—what? Ashamed. Afraid of his feelings.

And it was her fault. She'd helped widen the gulf between them that seemed as wide as the sea and as dark as the night sky. And they both knew what was needed now was time alone.

Slowly Ali made her way to the room. She had a hard time falling asleep. Even the gin and tonic didn't relax her. She had believed that she'd understood Sam when she met him on Indigo—tough and dangerous, out for himself. That's how she had categorized Sam Cantrell. She had used that knowledge to keep her distance from him.

But he wasn't like that at all. He was as vulnerable as Ali herself. Tears she had been holding back trickled down her cheeks as she thought about the sad little boy Sam had been. She wiped them away and stared into the darkness.

Once Ali had thought she knew Casey, that he was a good and honest man. She'd been wrong. Then she thought she knew Sam, a cold and unfeeling man. Again she'd been wrong.

The problem wasn't with Sam or Casey. The problem was in her own heart.

ALI WALKED FAST toward town, as if to get away from her feelings, or to get away from Sam, who was still sleeping in the hotel. But she barely noticed the blazing red hibiscus or heard the calling of yellow songbirds in the palms as she walked toward town. All her thoughts were of Sam.

She'd fallen asleep thinking of him; she'd dreamed of him and had woken up with his name on her lips. Who was she trying to kid? After all the denials and protestations, despite her self-warnings, the answer was obvious. Her heart and mind were filled with him. She was in love with him.

What a pair they were! He reached out, she pulled back. She moved toward him, he walked away.

Ali drank a cup of coffee at a little café near the harbor and watched the boats rock peacefully at anchor. The atmosphere was serene, but she was on edge and anxious, with so much in her life still unresolved.

She paid for the coffee and wandered back up the hill. Along the way she found a little side street that she had missed the day before. Deliberately she banished the hunt for stolen money from her mind in the hope that the casual approach would work when nothing else had. She would begin by behaving like a tourist and shopping extravagantly. Gwen's birthday was coming up, and then there was always . . . Christmas.

No matter how Ali felt about the holidays, she enjoyed buying gifts for her relatives, and Santa Luisa was a shopper's paradise. Of the stores that were open early in the morning, one caught her eye, a philatelist shop. She'd never really gotten over her interest in stamps, which Brian had inherited. She would bring some from Santa Luisa to add to his collection.

Ali pushed open the door, and the jingle of a bell brought forward a small bent man, shuffling as he came toward her, and then pausing and bowing low. "*Buenos días, señora*, welcome to my shop. I am Señor Benedicto, and I am honored to have the visit from so beautiful a lady."

Ali smiled. For all his years, Señor Benedicto had the heart of a Latin flirt. "Your stamps are beautiful, *señor*. I would like to buy a sleeve or two for my nephew, who has just started to collect."

"As in many countries, stamp sales and tourism keep us financially independent." The merchant pulled out a tray of stamps for her to examine.

"Maybe those." She pointed to a collection featuring pirates of the Spanish Main. "Or those."

Benedicto hesitated and then brought out another tray of seascapes.

"Sorry to take up your time."

"No problem, *señora*. Summertime is not a busy season for us, but when winter comes, ah, then we have more customers than we can handle."

"That's when the tourists arrive," Ali commented.

"Exactly," he said with a wide smile. "Our most wealthy tourists take up residence in the hills. But they also love to shop."

"I didn't realize they'd be into—that is, they'd be interested in stamp collecting."

He shrugged. "The wealthy collect everything, *señora*. Jewels, paintings, sculptures, wines, stamps and even women." He smiled slyly. "It is a competition of sorts for the most and the best. Many deals are made on Santa Luisa, both on the record and off."

Ali raised her eyes from the stamps with a prickle of interest. "Wealthy stamp collectors . . ." She thought of Sam's theory. Casey made a private deal to convert the stolen money. It could have been jewels, but why not stamps? "Have you heard of any unusual sales in the past few months?"

This time Benedicto's smile was one of pride. "I had such a sale myself around Christmas."

Ali's pulse raced. "For a great deal of money?" she asked.

"It is no secret. The stamp sold for over a hundred thousand dollars. A lovely lady from Italy bought it as a Christmas present for her husband."

Dead end, Ali thought. But she was on the right track. "Perhaps . . . some even rarer stamp . . ."

"Perhaps," Benedicto said.

"Rare stamp trading sounds exotic and romantic and maybe even mysterious. Or possibly illegal," she ventured.

"I hear many stories, *señora*, of the kinds of deals that are made." He leaned conspiratorially across the counter.

Ali nodded. "Big money?"

He lowered his voice. "There is a rumor that I have heard recently."

"Yes?" She felt like a fellow conspirator.

"About a private transaction that happened during the holidays."

"At Christmastime?"

He nodded. "Two stamps. A pair of the most valuable in the world, owned for years by a collector who winters here, a gentleman from Europe who found himself in need of cash. A buyer appeared."

Ali struggled to get her breath. "A buyer from—America?"

"I can say only that—I hear things."

"So he could have been from America?"

"Yes. It is possible." He was enjoying the little game.

"And the stamps could have been . . ."

"I am not sure, but I have a picture of the purported stamps."

"May I see it?"

"Of course."

Ali wanted to shout for him to hurry as he pulled one catalog after another from the shelf until he found the book he was looking for, flipped through the pages and laid it open on the counter.

"These are the stamps, *señora.*"

Sam had known what they were looking for—a purchase worth hundreds of thousands, something Casey could get rid of easily and then recover just as easily. Stamps sent to Ali. And there they were before her!

"He expected to come back for them," she mused aloud.

"I beg your pardon, madame?"

She avoided his question and quickly asked one of her own. "What makes them valuable?" Ali looked down at the matched pair, Queen Victoria and her consort, Prince Albert, each standing in a tropical garden in Santa Luisa, replicas of the stamps now in Brian's collection. "Is it the flowers?" Her hand shook noticeably.

"A nice touch of the artist's imagination, but no," he answered. "Some stamps are valuable because they are very old and rare or because of their unusual shape or exceptional beauty. Others have been printed with an anomaly of some kind. You've heard of the famous United States airmail stamp?"

Ali thought she remembered.

"The airplane that flies upside down?"

"Oh, yes," she said.

"Usually these mistakes are destroyed, but sometimes a few reach the public. As with these. Look closely, *señora.*" He handed her a magnifying glass.

With a trembling hand she managed to focus the glass.

"Look at her face, *señora*. She has eyes and nose but she has no mouth. One of the rarest of all stamps in the world—a queen who cannot speak even to her husband. Only two or three are known to exist and when Victoria's stamp is paired with Albert—well, the price paid of half a million dollars is understandable."

Half a million. She felt the blood drain from her face, felt her hands go clammy on the counter as she looked at the duplicates of the stamps in Brian's collection—the stamps from Casey's letter.

Sam had been right all along.

Señor Benedicto looked at her worriedly. "Are you all right, *señora?*"

"Yes, I'm fine." She took a deep breath. "I just remembered something. An appointment." She rifled in her handbag for her wallet. "Please, before I go, I'd like to buy a sleeve of, let's see, the pirates and maybe...the seascapes." She thrust the money into Señor Benedicto's hand.

"I will bring your change, *señora*."

"No, keep it, please. You've been very helpful, but...I must go now."

"*Señora*, I'm worried about you. You seem so distraught. May I call a taxi for you?"

"No, I can find one myself, thank you. Oh, thank you for being so helpful." She turned to leave and then suddenly whirled on her heel, leaned across the counter and kissed him on the cheek. "You'll never know how helpful. Never."

Then she darted from the shop and ran toward the main street, shouting for a taxi.

ALI RACED UP THE STAIRS to Sam's balcony and threw open the screen door to his room. He was sitting on the bed, the telephone receiver to his ear. She rushed across the room, shouting to him.

"Hang up, now! I have to talk to you."

Sam held up a restraining hand. "Ali, I'm on the phone to Government House. Someone is looking up—"

She grabbed the phone from his hand. "It doesn't matter."

"Ali—"

"Hang up, Sam! I know everything." She was still wrestling with the receiver, which Sam managed to get away from her and hang up. "I know! I know!" she shouted.

Sam stood and grabbed her by the shoulders. "All right, I've hung up on the poor woman. Are you satisfied? What's more important—are you all right? You look out of control, Ali."

"Yes, I am! I'm hysterical." She laughed wildly, stopped to catch her breath and then broke up again. "I know you think I'm crazy."

"Well . . ." Sam guided her to a chair. "First you better sit down."

She did as she was told.

"Now, what happened to you?"

"Remember you said hide in plain sight—remember? Well, that's just what Casey did. He hid the money in plain sight. I wasn't even looking for it, and I just—"

Sam handed her a glass of water, and she drank thirstily. "That's better. Maybe I can get my breath now."

"Don't rush, Ali. Take your time." Sam dropped to his knees beside her. "You found the money?"

"Well, not exactly, but I found the stamps, or pictures of them."

"Stamps. He sent you valuable stamps."

"They were on the letter! He bought them from a private collector who lived in one of those mansions. That was the answer, just as you thought."

"And you gave the stamps to Brian."

"Yes!" Ali stood suddenly. "My God, we have to call Tiger. Right now!" She surged across the room.

Sam was on his feet in an instant and grabbed her arms, pulling her back gently. "Sit, Ali." He laughed aloud at his command. "I don't mean to sound brusque, but you'll scare them to death. Keep talking. Tell me about the stamps while I place the call."

Her words ran on top of one another. "It came to me when I was looking for a Christmas present for Brian. Isn't that a hoot? I mean, it's ironic that Christmas would lead me to— Anyway, I went into the stamp shop, and Señor Benedicto . . . He was such a flirt. . . ."

"Ali, stay on the subject," Sam cautioned as he punched a series of numbers into the phone.

"I'm sorry, but Señor Benedicto started talking about all the wealthy people in the hills and the big money they paid for stamps. I remembered what you'd said about Casey converting the stolen money to diamonds or something valuable. I thought, why not stamps? So I talked to Señor Benedicto and as we talked, I was surer and surer. Then I saw the photograph. The stamps rumored to have been bought for half a million are the very ones I gave to Brian."

Sam raised his hand for silence. "Hello, Gwen. It's Sam. No, everything is fine. Ali is fine. I'm fine." He laughed at her response. "Listen, Gwen, this is very important. I want you to go upstairs right now and get Brian's stamp album, the most recent one that I was looking at over the Fourth. No, I'll wait. It's all right. Take your time. I'll explain everything when the album is in your hands. Okay. I'll hold on."

He gave the phone to Ali. "The stamps you saw in the photograph..."

"They're the same ones, Sam. They're in Brian's album."

"Then walk her through it. Afterward, tell her to lock them up in Tiger's safe. I'll call Jerry as soon as you hang up. We'll get some security people out there." He paused for a second. "Are you sure, Ali?"

"As soon as Gwen describes the stamps, I'll know."

10

HALF AN HOUR LATER, Sam and Ali were back on the balcony, another tray of fruit and drinks on the table between them. This time hotel room service had been summoned, and their luncheon now included sandwiches and salads. Ali ignored it all.

"I'm too excited to eat or drink or even sit still." She got up and paced the patio. "Can you believe we did it? We actually found the money."

"You did it," Sam said, narrowing his eyes against the noontime sun. "It's over, Ali, and you did it. I'm very proud of you."

"But you gave me the clues," she protested. "You were the one who picked up on the seasonal tourists and a secret deal. And you mentioned 'hide in plain sight,' which was part of Casey's plan."

"You found the stamps, Ali."

She stopped her pacing and looked down at him. "I never would have asked the first question if you hadn't given me the incentive to probe."

Sam took a long swig of his drink. "Okay, we did it *together*." He emphasized the word. "So the team of Paxton and Cantrell is back in business."

Ali leaned against the patio wall. "Yes, I've decided we work pretty well together." She drew a deep breath and started to relax.

"Now that the money and Casey are laid to rest, we're still a team, right?"

"Well . . ."

"Maybe we should talk about it. About a lot of things."

"Maybe . . ."

"And maybe we should wait and have this talk later tonight. Now it's time for you to celebrate, Ali, time for you to go out on the town."

"A celebration? That sounds wonderful! I haven't had anything to celebrate in ages."

Sam grinned at her. She was as excited as a child at Christmas. "You're on. Now, come on, sit down. Relax and enjoy your success."

She perched on the edge of a chair. "I can't relax. My mind keeps racing."

"You're still thinking about the stamps."

"What made Casey send them to me? That's what I keep wondering."

"Do you want to delve into it or just let well enough alone, let it all go? Maybe that would be the best."

"No, I want to understand it, Sam. You taught me that it was impossible to outrun your past. So I might as well face it."

Sam smiled. "All right, if you're determined. We'll never really be able to get into Casey's mind, but we can guess, and some things are obvious. No matter what his motives, you were his link, his safety and security, especially when the police were closing in. He knew he didn't have much time to convert the money. He'd heard about the stamps."

"How?"

"There's a grapevine among the rich, Ali. They know things we poor folks never could imagine."

"All right. I'll accept that. But I still can't understand why he sent the stamps to me when he could have put them in his wallet and headed for parts unknown."

"Parts unknown," Sam repeated. "You've answered your own question. Casey had no idea where he'd end up. Remember, he was fleeing the law, not taking a deluxe tour. You were the only person he could trust."

She sank back into her chair, eyes closed. "And he knew I'd never throw away stamps, especially not exotic colorful ones."

"I almost saw them, didn't I?" Sam asked. "On the Fourth of July when you came tearing into Brian's room and took the stamp book away from us."

"I was afraid Brian would tell you they'd come from Casey, and then you'd have questions. That wouldn't have been a festive way to begin our holiday celebration. At the time it seemed simpler to put the book away."

Sam's grin was wry. "The answer was right there in our hands. It seems so obvious now, doesn't it? Of course, if we'd figured it out, we never would have gotten to know each other."

Ali's eyes met his, and she felt her heart thump wildly. His eyes were so compelling, so intense that she was drawn into them, pulled toward him with an implacable force.

"I would have hated that, Ali, not knowing you."

His low, husky voice sent chills along her spine. "Me, too," she managed, looking away from him. The air vibrated with tension, and she struggled to keep her voice steady. "How did he plan to retrieve the stamps?"

"I guess he figured that when things cooled down he'd ask you to meet him—in Rio maybe, or Europe, somewhere he could convert the stamps to cash without attracting attention. You'd have all the money you wanted and could live anywhere, maybe even here."

"I never would have gone with him."

"He didn't know that. It's obvious from his letter that he hoped you would join him eventually."

"He was a criminal."

"But he thought love would conquer all. He was also a dreamer, Ali. You've established that yourself. And if you didn't join him, he could always sneak back into the country and retrieve the stamps."

"But how?"

"It's done every day with fake passports. I imagine he had a pretty good backup plan. He just didn't count on dying."

Ali shivered in spite of the insistent sun. "Now it's over, and you and Jerry can get the stamps to Westfield, and the company can sell them."

Sam leaned over and touched her shoulder. "And you can forget this." His hand was warm against her flesh.

"But not all of it, Ali. There's a lot I hope we never forget."

A delicious little tingle quivered along her skin, which Ali attributed to the euphoric high she was experiencing after finding the stamps. Adrenaline pulsed through her, and she felt more alive than she'd felt in months. Tonight was going to be wonderful, she decided. It was going to be the beginning of something new and special, a clean slate for both of them.

Sam felt his excitement rise. All kinds of fantasies played in his mind. Ali preparing for their evening together, Ali in the tub, covered with soap. Ali toweling herself, Ali slipping into her lacy lingerie. So many sexy thoughts, so many delicious possibilities.

In spite of the fantasies, he kept his words easy and casual. "About eight o'clock?"

She stood and looked down at him. "Eight it is."

"We'll start all over again, Ali."

"Yes, new memories for both of us."

SAM KNOCKED ON ALI'S DOOR at eight sharp. He felt like a schoolboy on a first date, his heart beating a nervous tattoo against his chest.

"Sensational!" he said when she opened the door.

Ali flushed with pleasure. "You like it? Really?" She moved away, turned and came back toward him with a model's walk, cool and haughty. "Just a little something I picked up for a few hundred bucks at the hotel boutique." She turned again, and the full white skirt wrapped around her legs, brushed her calves, settled at the apex of her knees.

Sam caught his breath, reached out, touched her waist and pulled her close. Through the tight fabric of her dress he could see clearly the roundness of her breasts and the outline of her nipples.

"The dress is wonderful, and you're gorgeous. But I knew that."

"You look great, too." She smiled up at him. "White pants, blue print shirt. Very tropical. Very handsome," she added under her breath.

But he wasn't listening. He was just looking. Ali turned away from the intensity of his gaze. She had been thinking of being with him all day, and now that he was here, her heart was jumping all around. From the moment he'd stepped into her room the tension had been there between them, electric, palpable. Inevitable.

She moved toward the mirror, anxiously glanced at her reflection and said, "I thought I might put my hair up." Her voice shook, and her hands were clumsy as she picked up her brush.

Sam stepped behind her. "No, please leave it loose." He took a strand and let it slip through his fingers. Ali's eyes met his in the mirror. She wet her lips with the tip of her tongue. She could feel the heat of his body against her back. Desire, white and hot, flooded through her.

He ran his hand down her bare back, and she shivered and gave a stifled little half moan. She felt his lips, damp against her shoulder, and then his tongue moving along her neck.

Her knees weak, Ali leaned against him. "Sam, we need to talk. That's what we planned. We should . . ."

"Let's forget all the shoulds, Ali. Let's start over. Isn't *that* what we planned? A new beginning."

"That's what we need to talk about . . . at dinner." Her words were choppy and caught in her throat.

"Oh, yes, dinner." He turned her in his arms.

She moved away toward the door, thinking they would be going to the hotel restaurant. "Then we can discuss—" she began.

He caught her arm and pulled her back toward him. She started to speak, but he leaned over and stopped the words with his kiss. His mouth was hot and demanding. She resisted it only for an instant, and then returned the kiss, as greedy as Sam. They tasted each other with a long, exploratory kiss that seemed to have no end.

Ali felt the strong pull of passion. It clung to her heated skin and sang in her veins; it caused her to cling to him, pressing her body close and feeling every muscle and sinew of Sam against her.

As the heat rose inside her, a pulsating, liquid warmth washed over Ali with a primitive need. When Sam lifted her skirt and slid his hand up along her thigh, she trembled in anticipation. He pushed aside the lacy fabric of her panties and insinuated his fingers against her moist warmth. Tremors of excitement danced along her skin. She found it difficult to catch her breath, to think, even to stand, especially with what was happening to her. Sam's strong arm held her up against him as his other hand roamed her body.

Somehow they had moved to the corner of the room, where they found their niche, a wall to balance against, a place for them to hold each other, give vent to their feelings.

He was whispering to her in words that were soft, demanding and erotic, while his fingers played with her, sliding slowly in and out.

"I want to kiss your breasts and suck on your nipples," he whispered. "I want to be inside of you and feel your softness . . . touch your body all over, lick you, kiss you, love you. Just like before, Ali."

She sagged against him with a little moan, and Sam leaned against the wall, holding her tightly. "You're making my knees turn to jelly, Sam."

"That's what I want, Ali. I want you to melt against me. Don't worry, I'll hold you up." He kissed her again and again until her lips felt bruised, and her tender breasts ached with desire as they pushed against him.

"I need you, Ali," he insisted.

"Talk . . ." she said, conjuring up a thought from long before. "We were going to the restaurant to talk and celebrate. . . ."

He cupped her behind in his hands and pulled her tightly to him. She felt the hardness of his erection against the fabric of her dress. A slow throbbing began inside her that intensified each time they kissed. And they kissed over and over, again and again.

"We can talk later, Ali," Sam said. "We can have that dinner later. Now's the time for action, and I'm a man of action, remember?"

"Yes, I do," she agreed as she fumbled with the zipper of his trousers, proving that she was as ready as Sam for what happened next.

Greedily their lips met.

THE SHEETS WERE RUMPLED around them, their bodies hot and slippery with erotic playfulness. Everything seemed easy and laid back. But Ali was still hot with desire from the lovemaking that had just ended. With a sudden movement she rolled on top of Sam and pinned his arms with her hands.

She kissed him thoroughly and then sat up, straddling him. "I knew I was right the first moment I saw you, Sam Cantrell. I thought you were dangerous, and you are. You make me do all kinds of wild and crazy things."

"Like turn the hose on me."

"To put out the flames," she said. "Even then I knew there'd be flames."

"And fireworks." Sam pulled her back down on top of him. "We were meant to make love, Ali. From the first."

Ali looked at him through the screen of her hair that fell loose and free. She loved his face, the hard lines of his cheekbones, his strong nose, the sensuous curve of his lower lip. She pulled herself up on her elbows and looked down at him. Her breasts brushed his chest. The sensation made her shiver as her swollen nipples hardened against the muscles of his chest.

"I love your eyes, Sam Cantrell, your green, sexy eyes that see so damned much." She kissed his eyelids and relaxed her grip on his hands. Then he reached for her, but she rolled away.

"Not so quick. I'm not through with you yet, Sam."

"Hmm. Sounds torturous."

"Maybe it is." Ali became suddenly bold and sexy. "It is—slow and torturous and leaving you begging for more."

"I'll always be begging for more, Ali, because I'll never get enough of you, not ever."

"You deserve a kiss for that." She kissed his lower lip and then his upper. "In fact, you deserve a lot of kisses. I'm going to kiss your neck, and then your chest. . . ."

She loved the taste of him, the salty warmth of his mouth against her tongue, and she loved the feel of his body against hers, the hard muscles and soft hair of his chest. She used her tongue to flick his taut brown nipples, and smiled at his inward gasp of breath. "Do you like it when I lick you there?"

"Oh, Ali," he said with a groan. "If you only knew."

"Good. I like it when you do that to me, too, but I just wanted to make sure." She moved her lips downward. "I also like this." She kissed his chest and his hipbone. "Do you?"

"Hmm."

She circled his navel with her tongue and then caressed his manhood, first with her fingers and then with her tongue and lips. She found herself giggling. "I can do this to you, but—"

"I can't do it to you!" He laughed with her. Then they both turned serious, not talking, only acting.

Sam pulled her over so that she straddled him again. His hands fondled her breasts, cupped them, rubbed them. Urgency prevailed. Hurriedly they moved together. She lifted her hips, he held her up, she settled on him, he filled her completely. All that happened so quickly that Ali didn't have time to respond or even to catch her breath. She only had time to feel the ecstasy as their bodies joined—heat and pressure, hardness enveloped in softness, endless spiraling pleasure.

Ali was crazily out of control and she never wanted the feeling to end. She closed her eyes and threw back her head, giving herself to the frantic movement and the spasms of exploding ecstasy inside her, lifting her, engulfing her. Ali called out Sam's name again and again as wave after wave of rapturous release flowed through them and made them one.

Sam held out his arms and pulled her to him. Their bodies, warm and slippery with lovemaking, merged together, arms and legs entwined. They struggled for breath, still kissing, longing to be one, not wanting to be separated even for a moment.

"I love you, Ali," Sam murmured. "I've loved you from the first."

A great surge of joy washed over her, and when she said the words, it was as if for the first time. "I love you, too, my darling."

"YOU'RE UP EARLY."

Ali turned at the sound of Sam's voice. She was on the

patio, leaning against the railing, drinking in the cool, crisp morning and the clear view of the ocean below.

"It's a wonderful day. I wanted to savor it."

Sam crossed the patio and swept her into his arms. He was barefoot, wearing only his trousers, and his chest was warm against her. She felt the comfort of the night before in his arms, the warmth of a body just awakened from a night's heavy sleep.

"A wonderful day, preceded by a wonderful night," he said. "We have something special, Ali. I never want to lose it."

"Neither do I." She nestled her head against his chest and luxuriated in the warmth.

"Then we agree...for once." He dropped a kiss on her forehead.

"That we do," she replied.

"So. That means you'll be moving with me to Atlanta."

Ali looked up, startled.

"As soon as possible," he added.

"Wait a minute, Sam."

"That's the next logical step. I can't do business from Indigo, but you can run the Spice of Life operation from Atlanta."

"No, I can't."

"Of course you can, Ali. All you need is a fax machine and a computer hookup, and you can do it all—publicity, advertising, merchandising. Tiger and Gwen would work with you on setting up an Atlanta office."

Ali stepped away from his arms and pulled her robe more tightly across her breasts. "I hadn't thought that far ahead. Atlanta," she repeated softly.

Sam frowned. "I thought you wanted what I wanted, Ali. For us to be together."

"Yes, yes. I do. Only..."

"Then Atlanta is the next logical step."

"That's easy for you to say, Sam. You're already in Atlanta. I'm—"

"Ali, we're running out of romantic islands. It's time for a reality check."

"But Atlanta..."

"Put the past behind you," he said sternly.

Ali looked up, surprised, and Sam realized that he had been too harsh. "Atlanta will be different for you now. Your name is cleared, and very soon Casey will be forgotten. We'll make a whole new start. Isn't that what you've wanted? This is about us, not past history."

"Yes, I know."

Sam looked down at her face, which was closed and anxious, and he felt a sharp prick of worry. After last night this wasn't what he had expected at all. "What the hell is it, then? It's not Casey, it's not the money. Is it what I told you about my life?"

"No, of course not. It isn't your past, Sam."

"Don't lie to me, Ali, please." Something was suddenly very wrong, and he didn't know how to fix it.

"All right. I did worry—I mean, I do worry about your past. You missed so much in life, and I'm not sure I can make up for all that."

He grabbed her and held her tightly against him. "Honey, I don't want you to feel you have to make up for what I didn't have. I want to start clean and fresh. Here and now."

But she didn't relax in his arms.

"Maybe there's more to it," she whispered, on the edge of tears. "You once told me I didn't trust myself. You were right. I thought I knew Casey, and I didn't know him at all. I thought I knew you—"

"Yes, remember that? You thought I was a crook, invading your island."

Ali smiled. She had certainly been wrong about that.

"So now you think you're wrong about your feelings for me."

"No, I—"

"Yes, you do, Ali. You think your feelings for me, your love for me, is misplaced. It's not, Ali. You know your heart and soul. You know my heart and soul as no other person ever has."

She looked up at him, her cheeks stained with tears.

"And I thought I knew you," he said almost sadly.

"You do—you did, Sam."

"Then what's the problem, Ali?"

"I was sure after we found the money everything would be clear, there'd be no more problems, and yet..."

"Sure we'll have problems. Everyone does. But we can solve them together. I want to live with you, Ali. I want to love you, marry you."

Ali's tears fell faster. "I want to love you, too, Sam. But everything's moving so fast. I need time, time to go back to Indigo, to think."

He cupped her face in his hands. "We've had plenty of time to think, Ali." He studied her face in the bright morning sun, and what he saw there caused him to step back, hands falling to his sides. "I don't want to cause you pain, Ali."

"Sam, I—"

"You don't know what you want. But you deserve to be happy, and I thought I could bring you happiness. Maybe I was wrong."

Ali sank into a patio chair, her head in her hands. "I do love you, Sam."

"Then go to Atlanta with me."

"I can't. At least not yet. We can't just rush ahead like this just because you want to. We need to stop, take time to think things out. We can do that on Indigo. Come back with me or at least visit me there on weekends. Let's take time to test ourselves."

"That's hardly the place for a test, Ali. Indigo isn't real life, any more than Santa Luisa is real life. This is our moment. This is our chance. I'm asking you to come with me, to live with me and be my love. For better or worse, Ali. In the real world."

Ali sat paralyzed with indecision. She thought of her cottage, its warmth and comfort. She thought of the haven it had been for her. If only Sam would give her time to think and get her emotions under control. If only—

"It's not fair for you to give me an ultimatum like this,"

she said angrily. "You're putting our whole future on this one decision."

"This isn't an ultimatum, Ali, and you know it. This is the next logical step in our relationship. Love is an act of faith. I have faith in you, in me and in our love. Do you?"

Ali couldn't answer. She had put her faith in love once before and watched that love turn to ashes. She knew it was absurd to compare those situations, but there was still the nagging feeling that it would happen again. "I need time," she insisted.

"Are you afraid, Ali?"

"No," she said immediately.

"Not of me?"

"No."

"Or of yourself?"

She shook her head.

"Then it's the past that frightens you." He looked deeply into her eyes, so deeply that he seemed to be looking right into her soul.

"I don't know," she admitted. "I can't answer all these questions now. When we get back to Indigo, then . . ."

"No, Ali." Sam's voice was tinged with sadness, but it was very controlled. "I'm not going back to Indigo under these circumstances."

"Please, Sam."

He didn't seem to be listening as he spoke quietly but determinedly. "I'll change my reservation. Fly straight to Atlanta. Wire Tiger to send my things from Flattop." His voice was cool, controlled.

"If you'll just come back to Indigo with me, we can talk this through."

"It's too late to talk, Ali. It's time to act. I'm not going to hide anymore, not from my past or from my feelings for you. I'll hold on to those feelings as long as I can, but I have to get on with life. We both have to, together or alone."

Through the haze of her tears Ali watched him walk away.

THE VIEW FROM THE WINDOW of Ali's cottage on Indigo Isle had not changed. But she had. As Ali stared out at the ocean, watched the waves lap the shore, she sat like a zombie. The screen of her computer was blank. Her hands had not even reached for the keys. It was an exercise in futility. She just didn't want to admit it.

When Gwen called out from the back door, Ali responded eagerly, turning away from the computer with relief. "I'm in here, supposedly working."

"Tiger and I have been worried," Gwen said without preamble. "We've hardly had a glimpse of you since you came back from Santa Luisa."

"I know," Ali admitted. "I haven't felt much like company." She took off her reading glasses and laid them beside the computer. "On the other hand, I don't like being alone." She stared out the window. "I never thought that I'd see Indigo as a prison. But I do now!" The words burst out. "It's not the same. I never was lonely here before."

Gwen sat next to Ali. Her face was thoughtful. "You miss him a lot, don't you?"

"Is it that obvious?"

"Tiger and I thought you'd come back from Santa Luisa on cloud nine. Casey's problems were taken care of, everything seemed fine. But since you returned you've been lower than a snake's belly."

"That's how I've felt," Ali said. "Oh, Gwen, I have to talk to someone."

Gwen sighed. "I vowed not to interfere anymore."

"I don't want advice. I just want a friendly ear."

"I'll be that for you, Ali." Gwen reached out and caught her hand.

But Ali couldn't remain still. As she talked to Gwen, she stood and paced restlessly up and down the familiar room. "Sam took a really big chance," she told her cousin. She stopped for a moment and thought about her words. "He told me all about his life—and there are some really rough spots. My reaction was . . . it was just awful. I got scared and panicky and suddenly decided he wanted me to fix things for him. Of course, he didn't. That was a wrong reaction." She momentarily stopped her pacing. "Is this making any sense?"

"Kind of," Gwen murmured.

That was all Ali needed. She launched into the rest of her story, her words pouring forth. "All he wanted was for me to take a chance, just as he did. To leave this island and live with him, to give it a try. We love each other and we should be together, shouldn't we?"

Gwen nodded.

"But oh, no. I had to run back here and hide like a scared puppy. I felt like he was giving me an ultimatum. I didn't like that. So I ran."

"Was he giving you an ultimatum?" Gwen asked.

"Now that I think about it, no. All he did was to lay out options. Either we're together or we're not."

"Do you love him?" Gwen asked out of the blue, bluntly.

Ali stopped her pacing. "Yes, I do. I adore him! I have from the first moment I saw him, which you very well know, Gwen. He's exciting and funny and strong. We've been through so much in these short weeks, shared so much."

"One more question," Gwen broke in. "Why aren't you with him?"

"Gwen, that's the point of this conversation," Ali replied in exasperation. "What if it doesn't work out? What if I hurt him more? What if I can't trust my feelings? What if I let him down?"

"So what if you do?" Gwen shot back. "None of us is perfect, Ali. Sam doesn't expect that from you, and you shouldn't expect it from him. Maybe some of the problem with Casey was that you always thought he was perfect until . . . well, you know."

Ali, who had begun to pace again, stopped short, hands on her hips. She glowered at her cousin. "I don't expect Sam to be perfect. I know his faults very well."

"That's good," Gwen said. "Next question. Do you expect yourself to be perfect?"

"No, of course not. Well, sometimes. Oh, hell, Gwen, yes, I do."

"There. We've hit upon the problem. Casey was your mistake. And you can't accept mistakes. But you should, Ali. Everyone makes them. Only you use them as a reason to hide from life. Isn't that right?"

"You're full of questions," Ali snapped.

"I decided questions are better than advice."

The two women burst into laughter.

"All right, here's another one," Gwen said. "What if it does work out, what if it's great?"

"There's no guarantee that will happen."

"You're not going to get guarantees, Ali. Everyone has doubts."

"Not you and Tiger."

Gwen gave a hoot of laughter. "Especially me and Tiger. Do you have any idea how I felt when he began to talk about giving up his law practice, leaving the house in Charleston, all our friends, moving back to Indigo to start Spice of Life? Can you imagine how I felt?"

"Sure I can. You were ecstatic. You wanted to come here."

"Maybe. But that doesn't mean there weren't doubts and dark periods. Change isn't easy, not for anyone. We had lots of rough spots."

Ali felt her arguments fading away. "But you knew Tiger."

"And you know Sam."

"Not everything about him," Ali argued.

"Do you expect to learn more sitting on your behind on Indigo Isle? Ali, I can't talk you into anything. You've always been impetuous and stubborn with a mind of your own. I'm not going to get drawn into an argument about the past, about Casey, about why you feel safe here on this island. All of that's just fog you've thrown up to obscure the real question. Look in your heart. Do you love him and want to be with him? Or do you want to stay here and hide?"

Ali frowned. "That's a loaded question."

"No, it's not. You could stay here and manufacture problems and live out your pitiful life for the next forty years or so."

"Gwen, don't be so melodramatic."

"Think about it, Ali. Sam isn't going to live on Indigo, that's for sure. He's going to be in Atlanta, and that's where he wants you to be."

"What about Spice of Life? If I lived in Atlanta—"

"Some people would say love is the spice of life." Gwen grinned at her own joke. "Okay, let's be serious. I'm sure Sam has given you this option. In Atlanta you'd do us a hell of a lot more good with PR and merchandising than you're doing on Indigo."

Ali sat back down at her computer, thoughtful.

"Meanwhile, Tiger and I are going to the Trade Mart Christmas show, and we have tons of stuff to do before we leave."

Gwen headed for the door. "Besides, I promised only to listen, not to give advice."

"But I need your advice, Gwen."

"I doubt that, but either way, we all have to eat. So come on up to the big house and have supper with us tonight."

"Sure, and thanks, Gwen."

It took Ali all of thirty seconds to make her next decision. Gwen had crossed the kitchen and gone out the back door. She ran after her. "Gwen, I'm going to the mart with you."

"Hallelujah," Gwen cried as she stepped into her car. "Tiger will be thrilled."

11

THE PHONE RANG FOUR TIMES before the machine picked up. Ali listened to Sam's recorded message, her heart pounding. His voice was soft and easy. There was no hint of unhappiness in it. For a brief moment, that disappointed her. Had she hoped to hear just a touch of longing?

The tone sounded, and Ali panicked. She had given him plenty of time to get home from work, and had psyched herself up to talk to *Sam*, not his machine. She wasn't prepared to leave a message. She gripped the phone.

"Sam," she said in a whisper, and then with slightly more volume, "it's Ali. I've been doing a lot of thinking, and I—" She cleared her throat. Might as well be honest and forthright. In a steady voice she said, "I want to see you, to tell you that you were right about so many things. No more running, no more hiding."

It was all right now. She took one more deep breath. "I've decided to take the advice you gave me weeks ago and work the Spice of Life booth at the Trade Mart. We can get you a pass to see your skating crab in real life." Ali hoped the attempt at humor wouldn't seem out of place. "So please give me a call. I'll be at the Zenith Hotel." She left the number, even though Sam could easily have looked it up. She didn't want to take any chances. "I'll talk to you soon," she said confidently, and hung up.

Her hand still on the phone, Ali said a silent prayer that he would call. She'd done everything she could. It was up to Sam now.

AT THE SPICE OF LIFE booth Ali assured the customer, "Of course we can deliver to your shops by October. No problem." She wrote out what seemed to be the hundredth sale of the day, handed the customer his pink copy and flashed what must also have been her hundredth smile of the day. He smiled back and went away satisfied.

"Satisfaction's our goal," she said to herself. Customers had been milling around the booth since the mart had opened at nine that morning, sampling the spicy gumbo Tiger brewed over a hot plate and then placing orders with a zeal that had given Ali writers' cramp. Her voice was hoarse from extolling the virtues of the Spice of Life line.

"What did you say?" Gwen asked.

"I was talking to myself," Ali replied. "I think my words were something like 'we aim to satisfy.'"

"Well, that we do. And I don't believe we could have done any better if we had dressed up like skating crabs, like Tiger suggested."

Ali laughed. "We certainly couldn't have written any more orders. Wouldn't have been possible. We were smart to opt for comfort in our crab T-shirts." They were wearing holiday green shirts emblazoned with the Spice of Life logo and a cartoon pop-eyed skating crab.

"Another good marketing ploy," Tiger said from behind the steaming gumbo.

"And they're selling like hotcakes, too. We are over the top!" Gwen handed out a few more brochures while Ali wrote another order.

"Honey, I need more onions," Tiger called out.

"The man couldn't get along without me," Gwen told Ali, adding with a hug, "and neither of us could get along without you. I'm so glad you came, Ali."

"Me, too."

Being at the Christmas show was a definite high. Even though the temperature hovered around ninety-six degrees outside, the multistoried mart was air-conditioned and dripping with make-believe icicles, in keeping with the fake Christmas trees, wreaths and mistletoe. Christmas carols wafted through loudspeakers, and half a dozen Santas strolled up and down the crowded aisles, dispensing holiday cheer and free samples from their overloaded packs.

The buyers were in an up mood as they shopped for their retail stores. That they were sold on Spice of Life was obvious from the orders that had been taken, T-shirts sold, brochures dispensed. During a momentary lull Ali stepped away from the booth, eyed it critically and decided it looked great! Their newly designed Spice of Life logo was clean and crisp, the colors popped brilliantly and the three-foot enlargements of the skating crab and trio of caroling shrimp decked out in Santa hats gave the booth a whimsical appeal.

Ali felt justifiably proud of her hard work in pulling the display together. She felt even prouder that she'd barely given a thought to being back in Atlanta.

After the stamps were returned, there had been a small story in the newspaper, but not even a mention on television. The Casey Bell affair was old news. No one cared anymore. In fact, Ali had been interviewed about Spice of Life in the media without even a mention of Casey.

A line was beginning to form at the booth, but Ali let Gwen handle it while she took a moment more to survey the crowd. There were lots of faces, none of them the one she wanted to see. Ali glanced at her watch. Still plenty of time. If he didn't appear today, maybe tomorrow, and if he didn't come to her, she would go to him. Unless he was out of town on assignment. In that case she would wait. As long as necessary.

More customers joined the line. Ali caught a glimpse of Gwen's frazzled smile and started toward the booth, working her way slowly through the crowd. A Santa with an enormous set of whiskers was directly in her path. She stepped to the right. He blocked her way. She moved to the left. He followed.

"Excuse me, but—"

She was cut off in midsentence as Santa swooped down and in one quick, fluid motion scooped her up and tossed her over his shoulder. She heard Gwen's voice over the noise of the crowd.

"Great glory, Tiger. Santa's kidnapping Ali!"

Santa was moving so rapidly through the mart that Ali missed Tiger's response, but she managed to give vent to her own anger, shouting at the top of her voice, "Are you insane? Stop right this minute and let me down." Her voice was muffled against the fleece of his bright red suit. It didn't matter. This crazy Santa wasn't about to slow down, certainly not stop.

And the crowd wasn't about to deter him. Clearly, from the catcalls and laughter of the onlookers, they thought this was all a stunt, a Trade Mart promotion, part of the fun and festivities.

Ali's muffled screams and flailing arms only seemed to encourage them. From her upside-down, disadvantaged view she could tell that Santa was taking her across the skywalk that arched over Peachtree Street, into a hotel on the other side and down the hall. Once in the hotel, he moved faster, almost loping along. Ali stopped struggling and concentrated on just holding on while she prayed that Gwen and Tiger had called for help and security was on the way.

When her abductor stopped in front of a room in the hotel, fumbling with a key, she really panicked. "Let me down! I'll have you arrested, you—you maniac!"

The door swung open. Santa strode into the room and deposited her on a king-size bed. He stood before her, resplendent in his costume: pointed red hat with fuzzy white tassel, fleecy suit edged in fur, shiny black belt and boots, the most formidable white whiskers and mustache she'd ever seen . . .

And the greenest eyes.

"You're crazy," she said softly.

Santa pulled off his hat and whiskers and tossed them onto the floor. "Crazy in love, Ali." He knelt in front of her. "Crazy over you."

"Sam, oh, Sam. I can't believe . . ."

"I decided that I would come for you in a way you'd never forget."

Ali shook her head in wonder as she looked around the room. "I can't believe it," she repeated, her voice filled with wonder. In the corner there was a huge tree, decorated for Christmas, with gaily wrapped presents strewn beneath it.

"They're all for you," he said as he followed her gaze.

"And the tree! It's perfect."

"And not easy to find in July. I wish I could tell you I cut it down myself, like your dad. I didn't, but in December I promise we'll cut our own tree and decorate it together. We could start our own traditions, Ali."

"It looks like we already have. There're even Christmas stockings."

"Hanging on the doorknobs for lack of a mantelpiece."

"And champagne."

"Cooling for us to share."

"You did all this?"

"Down to the very last bow. I'm surprised at myself, but once I started, it was fun, buying gifts for the woman I love."

"But why Christmas?"

"Why not? Isn't Christmas the time for sharing and commitment, for being with the one you love? You lost that, Ali, and I never had it. It's time for both of us."

"Oh, Sam . . ." She couldn't find the words to express her happiness.

He took her face in his hands and kissed her. "Christmas with the one I love, and I do love you, Ali. You're not going to run from me this time, are you?"

Ali melted against him, returned his kisses and tangled her hands in his hair as she pulled him closer. "I told you on the phone, no more running, no more hiding. You've made it Christmas for me, Christmas with the one I love. And I do love you, too, Sam." Happiness coursed through her. It felt so good to hold him, kiss him.

Sam sat beside her on the bed and cradled her in his arms. "I wanted to do more than tell you how much I love you. Words aren't always enough. I wanted to show you that I could change. Hell, I have changed. Look at me! Sam Cantrell, dressed up in a Santa suit on the hottest day in July, making a total fool of himself. Is this the cynical guy who showed up on Indigo?"

Ali laughed in remembrance. "Hardly. But look at me, Sam. Who would have thought I'd be dispensing Christmas cheer at the Trade Mart and loving it, or that I'd be kissing my very own Santa?"

She pulled him close and drank deeply from his lips. The familiar excitement of being in Sam's arms swept over her. She sighed deeply and opened her lips beneath his.

Finally Ali pulled away and looked up at him. "I was so afraid I had ruined things between us."

He caught her up in a bear hug. "Couldn't happen. I told you, we were meant to be. I want you with me forever, sharing my home and my life. I've never had that, Ali."

"You're a closet romantic, Sam Cantrell, masquerading all those years as a cynic." Ali smiled through tears of joy. "Santa," she said tenderly, "we're going to have a terrific life."

"And there's no better time to start than at Christmas, even if it is July!"

Where do you find hot Texas nights, smooth Texas charm and dangerously sexy cowboys?

Crystal Creek reverberates with the exciting rhythm of Texas. Each story features the rugged individuals who live and love in the Lone Star state.

"...Crystal Creek wonderfully evokes the hot days and steamy nights of a small Texas community...impossible to put down until the last page is turned."
—*Romantic Times*

"...a series that should hook any romance reader. Outstanding."
—*Rendezvous*

"Altogether, it couldn't be better."   —*Rendezvous*

HARLEQUIN®

Temptation

Lost Loves

RIGHT MAN...WRONG TIME

Remember that one man who turned your world upside down. Who made you experience all the ecstatic highs of passion and lows of loss and regret. What if you met him again?

You dared to lose your heart once and had it broken. Dare you love again?

JoAnn Ross, Glenda Sanders, Rita Clay Estrada, Gina Wilkins and Carin Rafferty. Find their stories in Lost Loves, Temptation's newest miniseries, running May to September 1994.

In GOLD AND GLITTER, #501 by Gina Wilkins, Michael Spencer, a down-on-his-luck cowboy and single father, still dreamed of his ex-wife. She'd left him and their child for her country music career, but whenever her songs played on the radio, he couldn't help but remember.... It was only after he met Libby Carter that he began to wonder if he could ever let go of the past. If he could realize what was gold and what was glitter?

What if...?

LOST4

HARLEQUIN®

Don't miss these Harlequin favorites by some of our most
distinguished authors!
And now you can receive a discount by ordering two or more titles!

HT #25525	THE PERFECT HUSBAND by Kristine Rolofson	$2.99	☐
HT #25554	LOVERS' SECRETS by Glenda Sanders	$2.99	☐
HP #11577	THE STONE PRINCESS by Robyn Donald	$2.99	☐
HP #11554	SECRET ADMIRER by Susan Napier	$2.99	☐
HR #03277	THE LADY AND THE TOMCAT by Bethany Campbell	$2.99	☐
HR #03283	FOREIGN AFFAIR by Eva Rutland	$2.99	☐
HS #70529	KEEPING CHRISTMAS by Marisa Carroll	$3.39	☐
HS #70578	THE LAST BUCCANEER by Lynn Erickson	$3.50	☐
HI #22256	THRICE FAMILIAR by Caroline Burnes	$2.99	☐
HI #22238	PRESUMED GUILTY by Tess Gerritsen	$2.99	☐
HAR #16496	OH, YOU BEAUTIFUL DOLL by Judith Arnold	$3.50	☐
HAR #16510	WED AGAIN by Elda Minger	$3.50	☐
HH #28719	RACHEL by Lynda Trent	$3.99	☐
HH #28795	PIECES OF SKY by Marianne Willman	$3.99	☐

Harlequin Promotional Titles

#97122	LINGERING SHADOWS by Penny Jordan	$5.99	☐
	(limited quantities available on certain titles)		

	AMOUNT	$
DEDUCT:	**10% DISCOUNT FOR 2+ BOOKS**	$
	POSTAGE & HANDLING	$
	($1.00 for one book, 50¢ for each additional)	
	APPLICABLE TAXES*	$_____
	TOTAL PAYABLE	$_____
	(check or money order—please do not send cash)	

To order, complete this form and send it, along with a check or money order for the
total above, payable to Harlequin Books, to: **In the U.S.:** 3010 Walden Avenue,
P.O. Box 9047, Buffalo, NY 14269-9047; **In Canada:** P.O. Box 613, Fort Erie, Ontario,
L2A 5X3.

Name: _____

Address: _____ City: _____

State/Prov.: _____ Zip/Postal Code: _____

*New York residents remit applicable sales taxes.
Canadian residents remit applicable GST and provincial taxes..

HARLEQUIN®

Temptation®

IS TEN!

Join the festivities as Harlequin celebrates
Temptation's tenth anniversary in 1994!

Look for tempting treats from your favorite
Temptation authors all year long. The celebration
begins with Passion's Quest—four exciting sensual
stories featuring the most elemental passions....

The temptation continues with Lost Loves, a sizzling
miniseries about love lost...love found. And watch for
the 500th Temptation in July by bestselling author
Rita Clay Estrada, a seductive story in the vein
of the much-loved tale, THE IVORY KEY.

In May, look for details of an irresistible offer:
three classic Temptation novels by Rita Clay Estrada,
Glenda Sanders and Gina Wilkins in a collector's
hardcover edition—free with proof of purchase!

After ten tempting years, *nobody* can resist

Temptation®

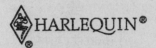